Omensford Series – Book 5

Exes & Enchantments

G Clatworthy

ISBN: 978-1-915516-25-1

Foreword

The Omensford witches first arrived in my writing in <u>Attack on Avalon</u> (book 5 in the Rise of the Dragons series), but they were too interesting to leave there so they had to have their own book. And so, this series was born, based around the fictional town of Omensford in the Cotswolds and the witches who live there.

A special thank you to my amazing typo hunters, grammar gurus, and plot pickers who got this story to where it is today. You are awesome!

If you want to support Gemma, you can find her on <u>www.patreon.com/G_Clatworthy</u> for exclusive first reads of new stories. You can also join her newsletter at <u>www.gemmaclatworthy.com</u> for a free short story based on one of the witches in the Omensford series and follow Gemma on <u>www.instagram.com/gemmaclatworthy</u>, <u>www.facebook.com/gemmaclatworthy</u> or join the reader's group on Facebook: <u>Gemma's book wyrms.</u>

Chapter 1

Fi gulped. Her stomach flipped with giddy nerves. Mort had offered to show her his world during the concert earlier that evening and now they stood outside his house. The old stone bungalow squatted behind a neat front garden complete with blooming flower beds and sported curved windows and a large front door that seemed too big for the house. The back half disappeared into a grassy mound, making it seem like a creepy fairy tale cottage, or maybe that was those nerves again. Grey clouds scudded above them, adding to the eerie atmosphere.

The last time she had been here, she had been too drunk to remember arriving, and too scared and hungover to take in any details as she was leaving.

Mort fumbled with the keys as they walked up the flagstone path. "We don't have to. If you'd rather…you can change your mind."

Fi linked her fingers through his and squeezed. She couldn't see much of his face in the dark, but his voice was tight, and she didn't like causing him anxiety.

"It'll be fine. I told you; nothing about your power will put me off. You've seen my destructive magic. What could be worse than that?"

He stopped and turned to her, cupping her face and forcing her to meet his eyes in the orange half light cast by distant streetlamps. "Your magic is beautiful, not destructive, and you've saved more than one life with it."

She looked away, uncomfortable talking about her own power. It was true. Her electrical magic had saved their friend, Effie, after her crazy sister had killed her, and just the other night, she'd created an electric fence to keep an enchanted pumpkin contained so it could be transferred to a nature reserve instead of taken for execution. But her power had hurt people too.

Fi had accidentally harmed her own mother when she had lost control during a lightning storm as a teenager, and…she had killed a witch. She hated thinking about it but it was a harsh truth and she wasn't sure that any good she had done could wipe that stain off her soul.

Stop moping. It was self-defence. Cressida, her familiar, spoke sharply in her mind.

Fi looked down at the small dragon-like creature at her heels. Her familiar sometimes seemed to be able to read her mind. It had been self-protection. Rationally, in her mind, she knew that. But, still…she had killed someone. Fi wasn't sure she'd ever completely get over that.

She looked back at Mort and forced a smile. "We're talking about your power, not mine. Come on."

Fi started walking again and Mort easily matched her fast pace with his long legs. He paused at the door, giving her more time to change her mind. Fi's heart raced. What was he so worried about? "You're sure?"

"Yes!"

Really, you're as bad as each other. Now open the door so I can get inside, out of the cold.

Fi rolled her eyes and ignored the wyrm speaking in her head. It was a mild autumn night, but her familiar loved the heat, must be something to do with dragon blood. Fi let Cressida hop in front of her and followed Mort through the door and into his house.

Her first thought was that he had decorated it in an older style than she was expecting from the doctor or what she remembered of his bedroom.

As if he could read her mind, he shrugged apologetically. "It's Dad's house more than mine."

"Mort? Is that you?" A rattling voice echoed through the house. The sort of voice that had smoked fifty a day followed by a chaser of strong spirits.

Which didn't make sense because Mort's dad was a doctor and knew the dangers of smoking. Fi tried to remember what he had sounded like when he had been her physician. Not like this, that was for certain.

"Speak of the devil."

An old man stepped out of a doorway carrying a cut-glass tumbler full of amber liquid. "Not quite the devil." His eyes twinkled as he took in Fi. "And who is this charming young lady?"

He stepped forward, tugging an IV behind him, until he was in front of Fi.

"Er, I'm Fiona, Fiona Blair, but please call me Fi."

"Charming to meet you, Fi." He placed the glass on a small table in the hallway and shook her hands warmly before leaning in to press his lips to her cheek. His breath had a tinge of whisky to it and something else, more medicinal.

"Fi, this is my dad, Hades."

"Come through, come through, it's so nice to meet you. Mort rarely brings anyone home nowadays; you must be very special."

"She is."

"Yeah, 'special' is one word for it," Fi muttered under her breath.

"Refill my drink will you, Morty? I want to chat to our guest." Hades led Fi into a sage green living room, still grasping her hand. In the dim light of the electric chandelier, Fi could see blue veins through his paper-thin skin.

"Are you alright? Mort said…" Fi trailed off. How did one finish that sentence?

"I'm sick. Yes. Dying, actually, but it's to be expected. We all go sooner or later. At least I know more about it than others."

"Because you're a doctor?"

Hades eyed her. "Ye-es." He sank into a faded yellow chair with extra cushions wedged over the seat for support. She sat too, on the edge of a three-seater sofa covered with matching fabric as Mort entered with his father's drink.

"Do you want one?"

Fi nodded. A drink seemed like a good idea. And she wanted something stronger than lager. "Whisky, please."

"A girl after my own heart. Bring out the Dwarven Fire Whisky, Mort. It's a special occasion!"

Fi decided not to tell them that she usually had it with diet coke.

"Are you sure you don't want to trade up to an older model?" The elderly man eyed her with a look he might have thought was charming or roguish. Fi forced out a laugh and repressed a shudder. Dr De'ath senior had been the family's GP until he retired, and it was weird for him to suggest he could be a boyfriend when he'd given her booster shots as a child.

"Dad!"

"What? Just joking. Got to have some fun before I die. Could be any moment."

He grinned as Mort left to find the whisky. Then his face went slack, and Hades rattled out a cough before slumping back in his chair. Fi leapt to her feet and yelled for Mort.

She bent over the old man, having no clue what to do. He opened his eyes and laughed in her face. "Gotcha!" he wheezed before slumping forward with a genuine coughing fit.

I cannot believe you fell for that.

"What's going on?" Mort ran into the room.

"Your dad, he…"

"Just playing a joke on the girl."

Mort glared at his father, left the room and returned balancing three glasses of strong-smelling alcohol. He handed Fi her drink. She sipped it, feeling the searing burn of the fire whisky as it went down her throat. She put her glass down on the carpet, feeling lightheaded. Best not to drink too much of that.

"So, you're serious then, are you?" Hades asked, taking a glug of his drink. Spots of colour returned to his pale face.

"What?"

Pardon, not what.

"You two." Hades waved a hand at Fi and Mort. "You're serious."

"Er…"

"Dad! Enough. I brought Fi here to show her more about our…powers." Mort ran a hand over his face. "Not for you to interrogate her."

"Ah, yes, the De'ath legacy. Good to know what you're getting into before it gets too serious." He swilled his drink around the glass, the sticky liquid almost climbing the rim. "Would have been better if I'd spoken to your mother about it sooner…" Hades stared over at the empty fireplace, his thoughts elsewhere.

A slurping sound drew Fi's attention to her familiar. Cressida flicked her forked tongue at the alcohol in Fi's discarded glass, lapping it down.

"Careful, Cress."

I know what I'm doing and don't call me Cress.

Three seconds later, a rumbling started deep within the golden wyrm's belly. Fi, Mort and Hades leaned back in their seats.

What are you worrying about? I told you, I'm fi...

Cressida didn't finish her sentence as she belched out a huge fireball straight at the ceiling. Fi stared in horror as the white paint blackened into a charred chrysanthemum.

"I am so sorry."

"Nonsense. Haven't had this much fun in years. Why don't you show the young lady our secret portal and I'll take this one outside for a walk in the garden?" With that, Hades unhooked himself from the IV.

"Dad!"

"What? Ten minutes away from the drip won't kill me, you know that. And exercise is good for me, isn't that what you always say?"

"But–" Mort broke off and tried a different tactic. "What will you do if something goes wrong with the wyrm? She's special to Fi."

"Pah. The worst she can do in the garden is burn down a rosebush, and I never liked the pampas grass we've got growing in the corner."

Mort gave a world-weary sigh and Hades gave his son the sort of triumphant look that Fi knew well. She'd seen it on her own mother's face often enough. Fi patted Mort's arm, commiserating in silence at the burden of having a headstrong parent you couldn't argue with.

Hades bundled Cressida up carefully, using the leather glove that rested by the fireplace, and took her outside. He wheezed in time with every step.

Left alone in the living room, Fi turned to Mort. He watched his dad go with an expression somewhere between worry and frustration. Unsure how to help with his emotions, Fi decided to distract him. "Portal?"

Mort sighed and downed his own drink, grimacing at the burning taste of the dwarven whisky. "I'd better show you."

Chapter 2

Mort led the way through the hall to the kitchen, an old-fashioned sort of room with copper pans hung from blackened beams. Mort had to duck to pass under some of them. He paused in front of a cupboard door.

"Are you sure you want to do this?"

Fi bit her lip, but she nodded. He opened the door to reveal a curving stairwell that descended into pitch black. The path to hell.

"Something like that."

Fi shifted from foot to foot. She hadn't realised she'd spoken out loud. Mort flicked on a light switch and the spiral staircase somehow got more sinister as shadows played on the stone walls. Fi swallowed and followed Mort down below the house.

At the bottom of the stairwell was another door. This one was heavy with cast iron hinges and a sturdy lock. Mort produced a large key from his pocket. Fi bit her lip again. Was the end of the key shaped like a skull, or was that another trick of the light?

The doctor placed the key into the lock and turned it. A dull clunk sounded from within the door. Mort leaned against the wood and whispered something softly to a knot that looked suspiciously like another skull. The door opened with an ominous creak.

Mort stepped inside and turned on another light. Fi crossed the threshold. In a room like this, she instinctively thought that the lighting should be shadowy candles to match the atmosphere in the cavernous space. Instead, a bare bulb hung from a fixture in the middle of an arched ceiling creating a weird hybrid of modern electric glare and ancient room. It was oddly disappointing.

The chamber was enormous, at least as tall as the bungalow, and the length of it somehow made the far wall both impossibly near and yet far away. The cobblestone floor was uneven underfoot, and she was glad she wore her converse trainers. Her breath came out in chilly clouds of steam.

A single silver sword glittered under the electric light, mounted on a stone that jutted out from the earthen wall. But what drew Fi's eyes was the large archway embedded into the wall on the far side of the room. Roots twisted and twined to create a semi-circular portal that took up most of the wall and she couldn't tear her eyes away from the sucking dark.

Fi hugged herself and took a step forward, wanting to see more. If she moved closer, she could see through the portal. What lay beyond? She had to know. Whispers caressed her mind, telling her to come closer and discover the secrets on the other side of the veil. Another step. The answers to all her questions were in reach if she would just step into the dark. Mort's warm hand on her shoulder broke her trance and stopped her from crossing the room.

"Careful, it can draw you in."

"What is it?"

"Our gateway to the other realm."

"It's…c…" Creepy was the word that came to mind, but Fi glanced at Mort before she spoke and saw a strange expectant look on his face, as if her answer really mattered to him. "Cool," she finished.

Relief passed over his features. "Do you think so?"

She nodded. "Yeah, it's like something out of a videogame. Cool." She repeated the word as if that would make it true.

He smiled, sending a warm fuzzy feeling through her body, and she was glad she had thought before she'd spoken.

"So, you go through that?"

"Only when I'm needed in the other realm."

"Oh." Fi couldn't think of anything else to say and she didn't want to voice her relief that he wasn't going to take her through into the realm of the dead. She turned, with some effort, from the mesmerising black hole in the wall to the only other object in the room. "What's the sword for?"

Mort took it down from its mount. His features sharpened with darker edges and shadows where before he had looked human.

Fi leaned away slightly, then shook her head. She was the one who had wanted to know more about Mort and his power. She had insisted they come when he had given her every option to change her mind and back out. Fi forced herself to stand still as Mort spoke.

"It's the symbol of my family's service. Generations ago, when gods walked among us, one of my ancestors agreed to serve Arawn, the god of death."

"Never heard of him."

"He goes by other names. Thanatos, they called him in Greece, or Mors, if you prefer Roman history. A servant of Hades, or Pluto, death personified. But he agreed to a game with my ancestor, or so the story goes, and was so impressed by her performance that he bound our family to serve him."

"What do you have to do exactly? Do you kill people?"

"Not people. He takes care of that. Or rather, nature does. But sometimes there is a lack of balance that threatens the mortal realm, like when that demon tried to come through…"

Fi nodded. An ancient demon had almost broken through, using a local kids' club leader as a conduit, but they'd managed to contain its spirit in a donkey that now grazed in her mother's back garden. She still wasn't sure exactly how that had happened. But the biggest threat the demon now posed was a nasty bite or kick to unsuspecting visitors.

"In those types of situations, my family brings the balance. We are defenders of the mortal realm." He drew the sword from its mount. "And this blade comes to me when I need it, when outside sources threaten that balance or when there is mortal danger. It can cut through anything, including severing souls from their bodies."

Fi raised an eyebrow. "Anything?"

Mort plunged the blade into a large round cobblestone, and the sword sank into the ground as if it were no more substantial than butter. He withdrew the blade and gazed at its dark surface. "They say that the god of blacksmiths, Gofannon, smelted celestial metal and forged the sword himself."

"Do you have to use it often?" Fi gaped at the thin hole in the floor, bending down to touch the stone that had been whole just moments ago.

Mort shook his head. "Not often, but every once in a while, when there's a soul in a body they shouldn't be in."

"Like Effie?"

"Effie was a special case. It was her sister who had displaced the souls and taken the body, so I chose to let Effie displace her." He sighed. "I expect Arawn will want to talk to me about that."

Fi's head swivelled to the portal. "Now?"

"He'll get to me when he's ready. One thing I've learned now that I've got the family guardianship is that gods work to their own timeframes."

She rested a hand on his arm, lending him her support. Being in thrall to a god sounded awful. "So, you're at his beck and call? Night and day?"

"It's not as bad as it sounds. It's not like there are daily attacks on the mortal realm." He forced a smile and remounted the sword on the wall above its black scabbard. The shadows fell away from his face and Fi relaxed as her Mort returned. "Anyway, you've seen what I am now; death's instrument in this world. I took the mantle when my father couldn't anymore."

He hung his head like he was ashamed of the burden he carried for his family.

Fi thought, then shook her head. "No, you're a guardian not a killer. This doesn't change anything."

He looked at her for long seconds, his brown eyes searching hers. "You're amazing, Fi, do you know that?"

She felt her cheeks heat at his searing praise and looked away. She wasn't amazing. If anyone was a killer down here, it was her. He tilted her face back up. "You are. And Fi, working with death has made me sure of what I want. Life's too short to waste on second guessing. I want to be with you, to see where this relationship can go. If you want that too."

Fi gazed into his eyes. Did she want a relationship? They hadn't worked out for her before, but maybe she hadn't been with the right person.

Her ex had always wanted more from her than she could give him, but she'd never felt that way with Mort. Should she shut out all opportunities for love because of one awful experience? What she did know was that she didn't want this to end, and she was willing to give it a chance.

Instead of replying, she moved her hands to his face and pulled him forward. As their lips met, a loud beep echoed through the cellar. Fi groaned and pulled out her phone, regretting the novelty ring tone she'd added to her text messages. She glanced at the screen and froze.

There, in clear black type, was her ex's name. Li was back in town.

Chapter 3

Fi cursed. Did this room have the power to conjure up ghosts of ex-boyfriends, or was her timing always this terrible? Either way, the mood was ruined, and her mind raced with reasons why Li could be in contact. Things hadn't ended well. Maybe he was sick, or dying. The room felt like it was pressing in on her as her head spiralled with unwelcome thoughts.

"Something wrong?" Mort asked.

"No. Yes. Maybe. I don't know."

"Anything I can help with?"

"Not unless you can get rid of an ex-boyfriend."

"I mean, assassination's not really my thing, but maybe I could make an exception…"

Fi snorted then sobered up. It probably wasn't a good idea to make a joke about killing an ex-boyfriend with someone who worked for the god of death.

"Did he…hurt you?"

"No, it's nothing like that. It was my fault it ended. Sorry, I'd better go. It's late and I've got reports to write up tomorrow and Cressida needs her sleep or she's a nightmare…"

"Right." There was a tone of disappointment or resignation or something in Mort's tone but, ever the gentleman, he said nothing else and gestured for Fi to lead the way so he could lock up. She scrambled up the stairs.

Back in the kitchen, she took a deep breath. Bloody Li, couldn't he be satisfied with dumping her? Why was he turning up now and ruining things with Mort? She needed to think, and she couldn't do that around the attractive, attentive doctor.

"Where's Cressida?"

"There you are! How did it go?" Hades appeared in the kitchen, a broad smile on his skeletal face as he panted from the exertion of walking outside.

"Good, really nice, uh, portal. Thanks for showing me, Mort."

"You're welcome."

"But I'd better be off, it's late and…work tomorrow. Just need to get Cressida."

"Yes." Hades looked over her head at his son, but she couldn't interpret their shared glance. "The little thing fell asleep, bless her. She's in there."

Fi scooted past Mort's father and scooped up her snoring familiar.

"Don't judge him too harshly," Hades said, his voice a mere whisper as he stopped her in the hall. "It's not his fault he was born to this."

"What? No. That's not it. I…Thanks for having me, I'll see you around." She darted out of the front door and into the night air, ignoring the looks that flew between father and son.

Cressida stirred as a chill autumn breeze brushed over her scales. *Where are we? Why are we outside?*

"I had to get out of there."

Why? What did he show you?

How could an animal inject such suggestiveness into its voice? "Nothing like that. Nothing bad."

Then why, pray tell, are we out in the cold instead of in the warm?

"I just had to leave." Cressida's silence crowded Fi's head. "Fine. My ex got in touch. There. Now you know."

The same ex who gave you that hideous owl ornament?

"It wasn't hideous…" Fi couldn't finish the sentence. The ceramic owl had been ugly, and Cressida had smashed it during her phase of destroying anything Fi owned that the wyrm didn't approve of. Fi was surprised she had any possessions left as Cressida had strong opinions on what she liked, and none of it fit with what Fi had.

Well, if it is that ex, I say good riddance. Cressida scrambled to get inside Fi's light jacket and out of the cold.

"It's…complicated."

The wyrm gave a snort and snuggled closer. Fi enjoyed the warmth of her familiar as she hurried back to her mother's house. With hindsight, fleeing a house on the other side of Omensford after Mort had driven them there had not been the best idea.

So if something's complicated, you just run away?

"No." That's not what she was doing. Besides, Li broke up with her. It was her fault he'd decided to end it, but she was the dumpee not the dumper. She hadn't run away from anyone. She eyed the grey clouds gathering overhead, wishing she had an umbrella with her.

She'd even take the hideous ladybird one that her sister had gifted her. Fi pursed her lips. She still had to get her sister back for that present, but she hadn't been able to find a garden gnome awful enough…yet.

A strange snuffling snort sounded from a hedge, pulling her thoughts away from revenge gifts.

Right. So, you're not running across town, instead of spending the night with the delectable doctor…

"Shut up."

I beg your pardon…

Fi clamped a hand over the wyrm's mouth and hissed for her to be quiet. Walking home in the middle of the night was a bad idea. Fi quickened her pace. Her magic swirled beneath her skin in response to her fear.

The wheezing got louder, and she hopped into the road to give the hedge a wide berth. Who knew what sort of creatures roamed the streets of the protected magical town?

Internally, she scolded herself. She was a witch. The daughter of the powerful Nell Blair, feared across the Cotswolds for her stern glare and sharp tongue. And she was a Magical Liaison Office agent, trained to deal with all sorts of terrors, or in training at least. She was one of the things to be feared here, not someone who jumped at a bump in the night. If she said it enough times, maybe it would be true.

You are a powerful witch! Cressida echoed her thoughts. *Stop acting like a scared child!*

Her familiar was right. And she wasn't running away from this. Fi narrowed her eyes at the bush and gathered her power. When the noise came again, she spoke clearly.

"Come out, whoever you are, or I'm blasting the bush. You have until the count of three. One."

The leaves rustled and something breathed noisily.

"Two."

Was that a laugh mixed in with the snorting?

"Three." Fi loosed a blast of her electrical magic at the shrub, charring its branches and blasting its leaves. A small squeak echoed down the empty street, and the hedge rustled. Fi stepped forward. A small hedgehog scurried out of its hiding place.

"Oh. Sorry, I didn't mean to…let me help you." She bent down, and the creature curled into a defensive spiky ball. Using her sleeves as a barrier against the prickles, Fi picked it up and placed the traumatised hedgehog into another garden with more cover.

"Sorry," she muttered again, backing away and heading back home. At least she hadn't hurt the poor creature.

Well, you showed that hedgehog who's boss.

Rain pelted down on Fi's head, and she picked up her pace, huddling into her jacket. Typical. "I'm not in the mood."

Clearly.

Fi took out her phone and swore as the screen refused to light up. Her burst of power had shorted it out and now she'd have to mull over Li's text until she could connect up her spare phone. Why couldn't her ex just stay out of her life?

Chapter 4

Fi woke the next morning to her spare phone blaring out its chirpy ring tone. She groaned, her head thumping as she came to. Why had she stayed up gaming when she got back? And why had she looked up Li's social media profiles? Everyone looked good on social media.

Too loud, Cressida moaned from her spot on the bed.

Fi reached for the handset and knocked it onto the floor with her flailing hand. Fi reached down and fell onto the soft carpet, pulling the duvet and the wyrm with her. Cressida squeaked. Fi swore and found the phone.

"Hello?" she croaked, her mouth fuzzy and dry. Fire whisky was never a good idea.

"Fiona?" Her heart sank as she recognised the gravelly tones of Detective Ledd.

"Yes."

"You sound like hell."

Fi made a guttural noise in her throat.

"Anyway, get to the town hall ASAP, we've got a situation."

"Wha–?"

"Dancing shoes. Hurry." The detective hung up.

Fi covered her eyes. Brilliant. Just what she needed today. What did 'dancing shoes' even mean? It sounded like some stupid joke, except Detective Ledd didn't have a sense of humour. She glanced down at the phone again and a new message caught her eye. It was from Mort.

Let me know when you get home x

Oops. At least there was only one message. If she were still dating Li, there'd be at least ten. But Mort knew she needed her space. She tapped out a quick reply.

I can take care of myself and yes, made it back safely. Fire whisky was a mistake though x

Her mouth turned up as she saw the three dots that meant he was already writing back.

Glad you're alright. I'm here if you want to talk about last night. Have a good day x

She sent him a smiley face and scrolled through her other messages on autopilot. She froze. There was Li's message. She still hadn't responded. What was the text etiquette for replying to an ex? Why did she even care? Annoyed with herself for giving it a second's thought, she tapped out a reply.

Sorry for delay. Been hectic at work. That was true. *Would love…* she paused, her thumbs hovering over her phone screen before she deleted love and replaced it with *like to meet up when you're in town.*

She pressed send. There, that was done. A reply came in less than a minute later.

Great! How about tomorrow night at Sorella's? I'll pick you up at 8 x

A kiss? Where did he get off putting a kiss on a text message to her? And replying so quickly to a message, what did that mean? Fi threw the phone onto the bed, annoyed with herself for agreeing to meet with the man who had walked out on her after two years. Even now he was trying to smother her with text kisses. It was suffocating and made her second guess herself.

She pushed herself up from the floor, closing her eyes against the burst of red sparks that exploded in her vision. Shower. She needed a shower.

The hot water made her feel slightly better, but the house had an evil sense of humour sometimes and blasted her with frigid water after a few delicious minutes under the steaming shower. Frozen, but thoroughly awake, Fi stamped back to her room to get dressed. She pulled on her comfiest t-shirt and sweatshirt coupled with skater style jeans.

"There's a case in town. Are you coming?" she asked her familiar.

Cressida groaned and curled up into a tighter ball on the duvet cover that still lay on the floor. Fi left her to it and headed downstairs.

Her mum bustled around the kitchen. "Morning."

Fi grimaced. Her mother was far too cheerful for her pounding head. She opened the medicine drawer and groped inside for paracetamol. She downed two tablets with a slug of water and put the packet back. Her hand touched a familiar glass bottle, and she pulled out *Madam Mim's Cure All*. She took a swig, wincing at the aniseed taste; it tasted awful, but the potion worked, and she felt its healing warmth spread through her body.

"Did you enjoy the concert last night?"

"Coffee, I need coffee."

Fi winced as her mum clattered around in the cupboard, selecting a mug. Was it always so noisy making a hot drink? She mumbled her thanks as her mother handed her a steaming cup of Goblin Blend coffee. Fi drank the elixir gratefully, slurping down the sweetened drink even though it was too hot.

A combination of the caffeine and the medicine took the edge off her hangover.

"So, did you enjoy the concert?"

"Oh, yes, Cirian was great. Where are they? I should say hi."

"Fiona, it's gone ten o' clock. Cirian and Effie were up hours ago." There was a note of disappointment in her mother's voice. "Where did you get to? The house woke me when you got back at half three."

Fi took another sip, considering her answer. Might as well tell the truth. "I went back to Mort's."

"Why didn't you stay the night?"

That was a good question. But Fi didn't think that telling her mother that she'd had a text from Li that had freaked her out and she'd basically fled the man that she may or may not be in a relationship with was a good idea. "I had to get home. I didn't have a change of clothes."

Her mother raised one eyebrow. Fi knew she wasn't fooling Nell. Her mother might care about having fresh clothes on a stay away, but Fi could happily spend an entire week in the same leggings.

"Anyway, good thing I did get back; there's a case in town. So I'd better go."

"Not without some breakfast, young lady."

Fi protested, but she took a slice of toast, which she lathered with chocolate spread. Aside from a bacon sandwich, sugar was the next best thing for hangovers. Fuelled up, she filled her travel mug and set off into town, wondering what 'dancing shoes' meant.

Chapter 5

By the time she got to the town hall, Fi regretted her choice of trousers. It wasn't raining, but a layer of water lay on the cobbled streets from the night-time downpour and her too long jeans felt like they had absorbed almost all of it, with dark tide marks up to her knees in the faded denim.

She eyed the café hungrily and wondered if she'd be able to sneak in and get a greasy bacon sandwich to help her hangover recovery. A noise from across the road made her sigh and cross over. It didn't look like bacon was in her future anytime soon.

Outside the town hall, she paused to take in the scene. A woman wearing bright red leather shoes danced a combination of an Irish style jig and a tap dance while a police officer followed her round with his notebook out, trying to take down a statement. In contrast to her exuberant bottom half, the woman waved her arms to keep her balance and shouted that she 'wasn't moving her feet. It was the dzraking shoes!'

A crowd of tourists and townsfolk fresh from last night's concert had gathered around in a half circle to watch. Someone had even set up a battered hat on the ground and bystanders threw in their loose change as if this were a performance.

Detective Ledd looked up and pursed his lips as he saw Fi. "You're here. Finally."

"I had to finish some things up first." Like getting enough caffeine in her system to deal with the detective. "What's going on?"

"That's exactly what I'd like to know. This woman tried on a pair of shoes in the shop and suddenly she's dancing. The shopkeeper thought it was a joke at first, but she couldn't stop. Then she waltzed out of the store."

"OK…"

"We got called in because technically it's theft, but there's clearly something magical going on." He laced the word 'magical' with a thick layer of disdain. "We've contained her to this square because she was heading for the main road. Sort it out."

"So, to be clear, you're asking me to stop the woman from dancing."

"Not the woman. The shoes! Aren't you listening?"

"Gotcha. Right, well, I have no idea how to do that."

"You're the bloody Magical Liaison Office agent. Figure it out." He stormed off to help the younger officer corral the woman. Fi stared as the woman shuddered, then opened her arms into a perfect ballroom dance position. She swept up

Detective Ledd into a sort of quickstep and whirled him around the town square.

Fi cut in, taking the detective's place and asked the woman to repeat her story. A string of Dwarfish curses later and Fi was reassured that the victim had no idea what was going on and had tried some shoes on and ended up unable to stop dancing.

As they finished their tour of the square, Fi handed the lady back to Detective Ledd for the next round.

Confident that the detective was occupied, Fi made her way to the shoe shop, figuring it was best to start where the dancing had begun. The owner stood outside, glaring at the spectacle across the street as she sucked on an e-cigarette, blowing clouds of vanilla smoke into the air.

"I'm with the Magical Liaison Office." Fi flashed her badge. "What happened?"

"I told the police already."

"They're not magical experts." Neither was Fi, but she was the closest thing right now.

The shop owner looked her up and down, then grunted in acknowledgement of Fi's credentials and introduced herself as Madeline Heel, owner of *Well Heeled*, the shoe shop. Fi asked her to go through what happened.

"Well, I was in my shop and this lady comes in looking for a pair of shoes for a wedding. It's a winter wedding, so she wanted something sturdy but special, you know."

Fi nodded along, but she did not know. The closest she got to special shoes was her collection of vintage converse trainers and she wore them for all occasions.

"Anyway, she tried a few on. No problems at all. Then we get to this red pair. She puts them on and starts dancing. At first, I thought it was a bit odd, but hey a sale's a sale, but then she won't stop and she's looking at me like she's scared and I'm thinking 'well she's the one dancing', and then she just heads outside. In the brand-new shoes, on the wet streets. Without paying.

"I raced after her to get her back in, but she kept on dancing, so I called the police. Those are two hundred pounds' worth of shoes, and I can't afford to lose that. What am I going to do, hmm? They're saying there's magic involved, but all I know is I can't sell scuffed shoes, so who's going to pay for them?"

"OK, so you didn't enchant the shoes?"

The shopkeeper gave her a look and took another drag on her e-cigarette. "Do I look like a witch to you?"

"You can't tell someone's magic just by looking at them, and you do run a shop in a protected magical town…"

"I am not a witch. I run a shop here because it's good business. Loads of tourists come through and they all want black boots, and the teenagers want gothic shoes and people like to try them on rather than go online."

"So, to be clear, you don't have magic and you didn't enchant the shoes or pay someone to enchant them to get sales."

The woman stared at Fi. "You know, that's not a bad idea…I could sell actual magical shoes" She shook her head "…but not if they're going to cause this much trouble. No, I'm not magical and I didn't pay anyone to enchant the shoes. Happy?"

Fi smiled in response to the shopkeeper's irritated tone. "So, can you think of anyone who might have done this?"

"It could have been anyone in town, couldn't it? I get witches and wizards in and out of my shop all day and the tourists and it was busy yesterday with the concert and all, it's not every day a famous popstar visits our town. I had a stream of people in and out. I had to shoo out some teenagers who weren't buying anything to make space for genuine customers."

"I'll need to see any footage you have."

The woman shifted from side to side. "Well, the camera's mostly for show…"

"So, you don't have any video of who comes in and out of the shop?"

She shook her head. Fi repressed a sigh.

"And before this morning, when was the last time someone tried on the shoes?"

The shopkeeper thought for a moment. "Last week. There was a Chinese girl who wanted something red, but she ended up buying some boots."

"And the shoes are on display? You didn't have to get them from out back?"

She shook her head. "These were out. I keep the size fours and fives out; they're the most popular round here."

Fi nodded and made a note on her phone. "So anyone in the last week could have come in and enchanted the shoes."

"I suppose, but I never noticed anything out of the ordinary."

"OK, well, thank you for your help."

Fi turned back to the dancing on the other side of the street. The lady had abandoned the detective as her dance partner and was now spinning on the spot like a dumpy ballerina. Fi sighed.

She had no idea how to stop the shoes, and her power would likely electrocute the innocent woman. She didn't have a choice. It was time to call her mother.

Chapter 6

Fi watched as her mother strode down the street like she owned it and surveyed the scene. She stepped forward.

"Hi, Mum."

"Dancing shoes…interesting."

"Any idea how to stop them?"

"I should think you need to get them off her feet."

Simple, but it could work. Fi called the detective over. "Mum thinks we need to get the shoes off her."

The detective levelled a stare at both of them. "That's it? That's your big idea."

"Have you got a better one?" Nell asked. Her tone had just the right amount of haughty scorn to force the detective to look away.

"PC Clark!" he shouted. "Get those shoes off her feet."

The younger officer knelt and made a grab for the woman's right foot as she jigged an Irish folk dance.

"Restrain her first, Clark!"

The woman span away and executed a stag leap that clonked the police officer on his head. A few cheers went up around the crowd; the British public were always willing to support a bit of slapstick humour on the street. A group of teenage girls giggled and pointed as the officer tried again, faceplanting the pavement as the dancer dipped into the splits.

One of the teenagers gave Fi a small wave, and she returned it with a smile, glad that Diane was enjoying herself after the tough time she'd had with her controlling thief boyfriend. At least that debacle was over, and Diane was being trained instead of using her powers to try to break into buildings. Fi snapped back to the present and remembered that she was here as an MLO agent. She schooled her face into a more professional expression.

"Interesting. It appears the shoes have been spelled to prevent removal," Nell said, tapping her jaw with a manicured finger.

"We'll see about that." The detective marched over to the woman, stepped over the prone officer, and dived for her shoes. She leaped over him and pirouetted, her face a mask of pain at the complicated dance steps.

"Stop! You're hurting her," Fi called out.

"What?" Detective Ledd shouted.

"All the dance moves. Her body's not used to them and it's hurting her. You can't just grab the shoes."

He stomped back over and the dancing quieted to a jazzy number with smaller steps. "What do you suggest, then?"

"We need to get her in the air, then maybe we can get them off."

"I'll help," Nell volunteered, and then she took over the plan. "You," she pointed to the detective, "partner her in a dance and try to lift her off the ground."

Detective Ledd tipped his head to one side, then called the police officer over and told him to partner the woman. He winced, but obeyed his superior officer and turned back with his arms out. The woman danced over to him, and they took up a slow waltz around the square.

"When I say so, lift her up. I'll provide some air to help, and then the detective and Fi can run in and grab the shoes."

Fi clamped her lips together, annoyed that her mother had taken charge with her customary ruthless efficiency, but she didn't have any better ideas.

"Now."

The policeman lifted the woman and her legs moved into an elegant position as he spun her around. Fi scrabbled across the uneven pavement, her trainers slipping on the slick stones, but she got close and grabbed the woman's leg as she kicked out. Fi clung on as they spun round, working the shoe off. The woman cried out in pain and Fi clenched her teeth as the kicking redoubled.

Her fingers found the clasp, and she dug in, forcing it open. As soon as the shoe was undone, it popped off the woman's foot with a sucking sound and Fi flew backwards onto the hard cobblestones. The small crowd clapped as Detective Ledd took a similar stumble with the other shoe in his hands.

The woman collapsed to the ground, dragging the police officer down with her and whimpering. Fi glanced at the victim's blistered, bleeding feet and grimaced. Detective Ledd shoved the shoe at her while muttering something about 'bloody magic' and called an ambulance.

The crowd dispersed now the entertainment was done. A teenage voice murmured something about it being like a fairytale as Diane and her friends passed. What story for kids had shoes that danced with no regard for the person wearing them?

Fi stood, brushed herself down and walked over to thank her mother.

"It was nothing, dear. But it takes enormous power to enchant an object that takes possession of the wearer. You should look into that."

Typical Mum, always telling her what to do.

"Any chance it was one of your lot?"

It was the wrong thing to say. Fi grimaced, wishing she could take it back.

Nell pulled herself up to her full height and looked own her nose at her daughter. "The members of the Witches', Wizards' and Warlocks' Institute would never misuse magic in such a fashion."

Fi's phone rang, saving her from a further tirade. She stuffed the shoes under one arm and checked the display; her boss, Agent Jones. How did the woman hear about this? She answered and tried to forestall any complaint about late reports.

"If this is about the dancing shoes, I've just stopped them, and I'll write up the report this afternoon."

"Dancing shoes? What are you on about?"

"Er, nothing. You'll see in the report. Why did you call then?"

"There's been a complaint."

Fi stayed silent.

"About you."

Chapter 7

"What do you mean 'a complaint about me'?" Fi's heart pounded in her chest as her memories took her back to her time as an IT support worker.

Complaints were always the worst part of the job, after dealing with people. Most of the time it had been due to her power surging out of control and shorting out the hardware, but she was better at controlling her magic now. She tuned back into Agent Jones.

"Someone you dealt with at the Haunted House has lodged a complaint about threats and excessive force."

"If it was that magic hating O'Riley–"

Agent Jones cut her off. "We take this sort of thing very seriously at the MLO, and I've got paperwork to sort out on this." Her boss sounded more upset about the paperwork than the complaint. "So, I'm sending someone down to supervise you until we can close this. Standard procedure."

"OK, I understand." Fi's shoulders slumped. She had just started to feel good about her new job, confident even in dealing with the problems coming her way, mainly trivial complaints mixed with a few murders, but she had solved them, and now someone was going to watch her every move and report back. "Who is it?"

For a brief moment, Fi dared to hope that it might be someone she knew. Maybe her friend Maxi; they'd had their misunderstandings, but since they'd cleared the air, she enjoyed getting his random texts updating her on tech advancements he was making on the job.

"A witch named Ursula Fortescue. I think you'll enjoy working with her." Agent Jones' voice had a strange edge to it. "She'll be at the B&B tomorrow morning." The phone line went dead.

Fi stared at her handset. Brilliant. Just what she needed, a supervisor to get in her way while she investigated some stupid dancing shoes. She rubbed her forehead, the earlier headache coming back in full force.

"Everything alright?" Nell asked, concern for her daughter crinkling her forehead.

"You've got a new guest at the B&B, someone from work's coming over tomorrow."

"Excellent. How long are they staying for?"

"As long as it takes."

Her mother gave her a look.

"I don't know how long she'll be here, OK?"

"Forget I asked."

"Sorry Mum, it's just work stuff."

"Of course. Can I help at all?"

Fi was about to turn her mother down, but she paused. She knew nothing about enchantments; her magic didn't work that way and she hadn't paid much attention in the magic classes at school, but her mother had years of experience. "Actually, can you help me figure out the enchantment on the shoes?"

Nell swallowed. "You want my help?"

Fi shifted in her converse trainers. "I mean, yeah, if you want."

"You never ask me for help."

"If you don't want to, it's fine."

"I didn't say that. I'm glad you still need your mother for something."

"You know I'll always need you, Mum. Who else makes a roast dinner like yours?" Fi joked, deflecting the emotion of the moment, unable to allow herself even a tender moment with her mother.

Nell frowned and held her hands over the shoes. "All I can tell is that it's a powerful magic user."

"How do you do that?"

Her mother turned her hands over and waved them over the shoes again. "I concentrate and sense the magic. You try."

Fi held her own hands over the shoes and her brow creased as she focused. She felt nothing, only the crackling sensation of her own magic. She shook her hands, disappointed, and frustrated that her power leaned towards destruction. She couldn't even sense enchantments.

"Never mind, dear, not everyone can do everything. Let's try the library."

Chapter 8

Fi glared at the red shoes that seemed so warm and innocent in the soft light of the library at the Bed & Breakfast that doubled as the family's home. Two books floated past, exchanging places on the built-in shelves.

"What exactly are we looking for?" Fi asked.

"Enchantments, for one."

"And shoes, for two?"

"That would be a good start. Do you want to do the honours, or shall I?"

Fi gestured to let her mother know that she should go ahead. Nell had a stronger link with the house and the library responded to her requests better than Fi's.

Her mother walked to the centre of the room, the warm light turning her white hair a soft blonde colour in its severe chignon. She spoke loudly and clearly, asking the library for books on enchantments and enchanted shoes. An expectant pause followed as the house considered her request, before a low papery rustling sounded through the room.

Books slid to the edge of the shelves and hovered, vibrating slightly with the house's magic. Fi snatched the ones closest to her before they could hit the floor, while her mum collected the rest, both of them used to the strange magic of the library.

"A book of fairy tales? How's that going to help?"

"The house provides what it thinks we need based on what we ask for. There must be a link somewhere. Why don't you open it and have a look?"

Fi placed the rest of the books on the low table in front of the one wall that wasn't lined with bookshelves and flicked through the fairy tale stories. These weren't the tales that were normally told to children by humans. These were the grittier, older stories, closer to the truth and recorded as cautionary tales of magic gone wrong, or in some grim cases, humans punished.

Fi shuddered at one illustration that captured a transformation partway between a swan and a person, their face twisted in pain as their bones popped into new shapes. She turned the pages until she stopped on a story about shoes. Seven-league boots that allowed their owner to travel vast distances with one step.

A good idea in theory, but only if the magic was exactly right, otherwise the user's body would split in two as half went with the front leg and the rest stayed behind. Fi grimaced at the illustration that went with that story. No wonder the boots had fallen out of favour, and everyone used safer transport methods, like aeroplanes, or broomsticks, or, in her case, her X-5000 vacuum cleaner.

But someone had enchanted the shoes to dance, not travel across countries with a single step. She carried on reading.

"Here. Look, there's a tale about red dancing shoes here." Looked like those kids were right. Her mother looked up from a green leather book, turning to listen as Fi read out the story.

"Once upon a time in Denmark, there was a girl named Karen. She had everything that a child could wish for, and her doting parents granted her every desire. One day, she asked for a pair of red shoes, having seen a pair in the window of a local cobbler's shop." Fi looked up. "Sound familiar?"

Her mother gestured for her to continue, and Fi went back to the gothic text.

"She pleaded and begged, and the girl's mother had a pair custom made with red silk and leather at great expense. Karen was overjoyed with the gift and wore the shoes everywhere. She wore them inside, tapping on the floors with the hard soles, and she wore them outside, laughing as her dance steps kicked mud at local villagers who were too poor to complain to her wealthy family for fear of retribution.

"A local warlock, Hans, cautioned the child to beware of her vanity lest she be punished for it, but she would not listen and instead danced through a puddle, coating him with water. Hans did nothing at that time.

"The final straw came when a local dignitary died. He had been well loved by the townsfolk and was a good friend to Hans. Everyone turned out for his funeral in dark mourning clothes, all except Karen. The prideful girl wore the bright red shoes with her black dress. A villager remarked that she looked like she was 'dressed for dancing rather than a funeral' and instead of hanging her head modestly, she laughed and twirled, posing in her shoes and taking a few dancing steps.

"Hans could not let the insult to his departed friend go unpunished, so he cursed the shoes to dance forevermore. Karen laughed at his curse and did a few steps, but when she tried to stop, the shoes kept dancing with her feet tightly laced inside.

"Her parents screamed and dragged their daughter away, still dancing. Two days later, they came to Hans' door, begging him to remove his curse. They had tried everything to remove the shoes and stop the dancing, but to no avail. Karen was weak, her body unable to get rest as she danced even in her sleep. But Hans refused, even when the girl herself waltzed to his door and begged his forgiveness.

"The girl spat at his feet after his refusal and told him that he was no longer welcome in the town, to which Hans replied that he would leave. The next day, when the family returned to once again beg him to remove the curse, the warlock was gone.

"In desperation, after more than a month of constant dancing which ravished her body, Karen begged for her feet to be amputated. Reluctantly, her parents agreed and tied her down as the doctor chopped off her feet, still tapping in the red shoes.

"All looked on in horror as her amputated feet kept dancing, trapped by the warlock's magic in the shoes. Karen spent the rest of her days hobbling on carved wooden feet, supported by crutches, but she was never allowed to forget her pride as her severed feet danced on ahead of her wherever she went, stuck in her red dancing shoes.

"And so, always respect the dead and beware of pride before a fall." Fi finished with the moral of the tale. "Ugh, that's awful. And look at this picture. Those feet are rotting, and they still danced around the town."

Nell sighed. "And that's why magic users get a bad name." She took the book from Fi and riffled through the pages. "Hans travelled round Denmark dolling out curses like they were sweets at any supposed slight to him or a friend. I'd forgotten about the red shoes."

"So, are these shoes revenge? It sounded like the lady in the shop just tried them on. There wasn't any way to know that she'd pick those shoes."

"Perhaps."

"Unless it was revenge on the shopkeeper, but that doesn't make sense; she wouldn't try on her own shoes. The only way it would hurt the shopkeeper was the money she lost on the sale. And cursing shoes seems extreme for a couple of hundred quid." Fi rubbed her forehead. She enjoyed problem solving, but too many pieces of the puzzle were missing.

"All I know is that these shoes have a powerful enchantment on them, to possess a body while the magic wielder isn't in sight."

Fi tapped her fingers on the table. "Is sight important? There were a lot of people watching the dance."

"It can be. It depends on the type of enchantment or curse. If a witch is channelling magic into the spell, it's more powerful than if it's a resting spell."

"So, it's a witch, then? Not a warlock."

Nell held her hands over the shoes and waved them in a complicated motion. The red leather sparkled, and her mother nodded. "I'd say it's witch magic, but it's no one I'm familiar with."

Fi nodded and made a note on her phone before going back to turning pages.

Chapter 9

Fi stared at her computer screen. The blank report stared back at her. She wanted to get a head start and earn some brownie points, but the reality was she knew next to nothing, despite spending most of the day in the library with her mother.

She sighed and filled out the easy fields; name of incident, date, name of agent, blah, blah, blah. Then she tapped in what she had found, grimacing as she referenced the fairy tale. It wasn't hard evidence, but it was too close to what had happened for her to ignore.

Can't you type more quietly?

"You've slept most of the day. What's it you're always telling me about getting up and seizing the day?"

I don't believe I've ever said that.

Fi swivelled in her ergonomic gaming chair and stared at her familiar. Cressida returned her gaze with unblinking reptile eyes.

"Unbelievable."

Fi turned back to the screen and finished filling out the scant information she had before closing the report and opening up the separate browser she kept just for gaming. Fi needed to wind down, and there was no better way than shooting at something, except none of her friends were online and it wasn't the same gaming without them. She closed down the browser and huffed out another loud sigh.

Go downstairs and bake if you're so wound up.

"Fine, I'll leave you to sleep, your majesty."

Cressida eyed the witch. *Good. And my title is 'Lady' not 'Queen'.*

Fi left the room, rolling her eyes. What sort of name was Lady Cressida Charmington for a pet? Or a familiar. Goody Winships, Cressida's previous witch, had a lot to answer for…although, Fi didn't know whether Goody had named the wyrm or if someone else had.

She frowned. Her and Cressida had been bonded for over a year, and she still didn't know some of the basic things about her. She should ask. Fi turned to march back in the room right then before her shoulders slumped.

Now wasn't the time. She was too keyed up about the supervisor coming tomorrow and Cressida wanted to sleep. One thing she had learned was that it was best not to try to engage the wyrm when she was sleepy, or hungry, or in a bad mood, which meant there was about a ten-minute window each day where they could have a civil conversation.

Instead, Fi continued downstairs and pulled out her pans, ready for baking. She mixed the dough by hand, having given up on electric mixers years ago thanks to her unpredictable power that shorted out anything electronic when she was in a bad mood, and, since she baked when she was stressed, that meant she had blown up more mixers than she liked to remember. Besides, using her muscles to knead the dough helped get the tension out.

She made a batch of scones out of habit, and made a note to drop them off at the café tomorrow. She slid the baking tray into the oven with satisfaction and made herself a hot chocolate while she waited, stirring the milk over the stove.

"That smells delicious. Mind if I join you?"

"Not at all, Effie, come on in."

"Thanks, love."

Fi added more milk and some of the rich chocolate mix she loved into the pan.

"Any reason you're baking? Not that I'm complaining. We always love selling the scones at the café."

"Just nervous, I guess." Fi kept her back to the older witch. Even though she felt more comfortable talking to Effie than almost any other person, she still had a hard time sharing her worries and tended to keep them to herself.

"Want to talk?"

"The MLO's sending over someone to supervise me for a while. I just don't know what to expect."

"Anyone I know?"

"Ursula someone."

"Fortescue?"

"That's her."

"She's lovely. I think she'll help you a lot." Now Effie was in her new, younger body, Fi forgot that she was old enough to have met practically everyone in the witching community. "Your mum went to school with her."

Fi spun round, intrigued. "Really?"

"Yes, she's a local girl, although she lives in London now. I think you'll get on well."

"Huh." Fi couldn't think of anything else to say.

"Is that all that's bothering you?" Effie could be annoyingly perceptive.

"Is that your psychic powers talking?"

"No, it's your friend talking."

Fi shifted guiltily; Effie hadn't deserved that. She poured the steaming hot chocolate into two mugs and passed one to Effie. She sipped hers until it was clear that Effie wasn't going to break the silence.

"It's just…Li got in touch," Fi mumbled over the rim of her mug.

Effie's eyes narrowed, but she kept silent.

"And I agreed to meet him for dinner tomorrow, and I'm not even sure I want to go, or why I said yes, and I messed everything up with Mort yesterday and…maybe I'm just not meant for relationships." There. She'd said it and voiced the worry that huddled deep inside her subconscious, setting her darkest fear free into the world.

She got on better with computers and online avatars than with people and maybe that was the best she could hope for. Everyone said she was 'different' and that was the politest word they used.

It wasn't like she was looking for a relationship when Mort showed up in her life with his stupid, handsome face and great personality and his honest way of caring about her. She couldn't figure out what he saw in her, and it bugged her. A lot.

"I see. Well, for what it's worth, I think you have a lot of strong relationships in your life."

Yeah. With her online friends.

"With your family."

Fi blinked. Could Effie read minds? "I think you're mixing me up with my sister."

"I may be over ninety, but my mind is still sharp, and don't you forget it." Effie gave her a stern look over the top of her mug, and Fi mumbled an apology. "Agatha may count most of the village as her friends, but not all of us need that many connections. You have deeper relationships with fewer people, and that's perfectly fine."

"Maybe, but Li left because I couldn't commit to him like he wanted, like a normal person could."

"Maybe you should have this conversation with Li and get some closure. It will do you good and remember, you don't have to push people away. You worry about hurting people with your magic too much. You can learn to live with people. You're back with your mother for goddess' sake and I was there for your troubled teenage years where you two got along worse than a pair of harpies with a head cold. And who knows, maybe you'll find someone you can trust enough to rely on."

"Have you seen that? Will I get closure? Can you promise I won't hurt anyone?" Fi couldn't keep the hope out of her voice. If Effie had had a vision of her getting closure, then she could stop second guessing herself.

The older witch shook her head. "No visions, but that doesn't mean I'm not right."

Fi nodded, but inside her stomach still roiled. Effie couldn't promise her anything. They drank in companionable silence while the scones browned in the oven. But maybe she had to try, at least, if she didn't want to be alone forever. Maybe it wouldn't be such a bad thing to meet with Li. After all, she was a different person now. One who'd kept a job for over a year and had faced the worst her magic could do and still strove to control it and use it to help people.

Maybe she would get some closure and then she could stop running from her budding relationship with someone who actually cared about her. If she didn't mess it up.

Chapter 10

Fi woke up early the next day with a sick feeling in her stomach. She couldn't blame it on the aftereffects of the fire whisky from the other night; not even dwarven drink was that strong. It was nerves. The Magical Liaison Office supervisor was due today.

Stop worrying. It will be fine. You didn't do anything wrong. This is just procedure.

"I hope you're right."

Of course I'm right.

Fi was about to grab some clothes from the pile on the floor when her wardrobe doors shot open. She took the house's hint and got dressed in a plain black sweater dress and clean leggings. The floorboards rattled under her bare feet.

"Alright, I'll tidy up." Fi snatched up the laundry from the floor and headed downstairs, cursing every time a stray sock fell from the voluminous pile.

A text came in and she fumbled with the washing, dropping a couple of socks as she read it in the hall.

Read your report. Dancing shoes, sounds tutu exciting! Jones told me about Ursula. Good luck and hope you're well. Maxi x

Fi groaned at the terrible pun, but a smile played on her face as she responded.

It's all go go boots here.

She pushed open the kitchen door and stopped. A pair of dirty pants fell to the floor. There, across from her mum, drinking tea from a china cup with Effie and Cirian, the elven popstar, was an unfamiliar witch. Fi swallowed and forced her feet forward.

"Ah, you must be Fiona." The witch stood and held out her hand. "Lovely to meet you."

"Er…" Fi slunk forward and shook the outstretched hand, wincing slightly at the firm grip. The rest of the washing slipped to the floor. "You too, Mrs Fortescue. Call me Fi."

She bent over and retrieved the dirty clothes.

"Really? Sounds like a dog's name. Whatever you prefer, though. And you can call me Ursula." The witch sat back down and beamed around the room. "I've read all your reports, and it was so lovely to get a call to come back to the old town, relive the glory days and all that. Did your mother ever tell you about the time we turned the grass blue? Caused quite the stir, especially since we couldn't turn it back. Had to wait for the darn stuff to grow out." She brayed out a laugh.

Nell pursed her lips and drank her tea. Fi had never seen her mother so uncomfortable.

"Anyway, no time to waste. I want to see what you can do."

"Er, sure, sounds good. Let me put the washing on, and I need to drop something off at the café, then we can go."

"Excellent, I'll join you. I can't wait to see the old café. I used to work there when I was a gal. Your great aunt ran the shop then." Ursula nodded to Effie, then frowned. "She was called Effie too."

"It's a family name," Effie replied smoothly, sipping her own drink.

Fi poured herself a coffee. So, Effie was continuing the ruse that she was her own great niece to avoid explaining how she came to have a different body. Fi didn't blame her.

It was hard to understand that Effie's sister had been killing young women and stealing their bodies for decades, and then had tried to murder Effie to get a special crystal ball. Mort and Liv had rescued Effie's soul by travelling to the dream realm and transferred it into her sister's stolen body. It made Fi's head spin just thinking about it.

Fi shook her travel cup. "Ready when you are."

"Well, it's been lovely catching up, Nelly. So glad I'm staying here, and we can have a proper chat tonight, just like old times."

Ursula didn't seem to notice her mother's wince.

"Good luck, Fi, we'll be gone when you get back." Effie smiled at her.

"Gone?"

"Cirian's got to be back in London to record his latest album and I thought I might travel again. The Swiss Alps are lovely for Christmas, and now I can ski again, I might even beat my – I mean, the record descent down La Chavenette. Anyway, I'll say goodbye now, love." Effie stood and pulled her into a hug. "Remember, you don't have to push people away," she whispered softly enough so only Fi could hear her.

Fi wrapped her arms around the old woman and hugged her tightly. "Stay in touch."

"I will. Now, go on, before I start crying."

Fi grinned and headed out of the door, the tub of scones under one arm and travel mug filled with Goblin Blend coffee in her hand.

Ursula stopped just outside. "Bring your familiar." She carried on down the path.

Fi called Cressida, and they followed the older witch into the garden with the wyrm grumbling good-naturedly about having to leave the warmth of the kitchen. Ursula stood in front of the fluffy donkey that lived in the back garden, one hand outstretched as if to stroke his fuzzy ears.

"I wouldn't…" Fi sprinted across the grass, skidding to a halt next to the older witch.

Ursula gave her a puzzled look, her hand still held out. Timaeus whipped his head up and swiped at her stubby fingers with his teeth. Ursula screamed and backed up so fast that she fell over. The demon donkey took a step forward, his red eyes glinting with menace.

Fi dropped the tin of scones and placed herself in between the two, her hands crackling with electricity. "Come on, Timmy, play nice."

"My name is Timaeus," he ground out, "and she started it."

"That's no excuse to bite someone." Fi kept her hands pointed at the donkey and glanced over her shoulder at Ursula, who scrambled to her feet. "Sorry, he's a bit tetchy. I'd say it's because he's a demon's essence trapped in a donkey's body, but I expect he's always been a grump. Haven't you, Tim-eh-*ass*?" Fi deliberately mispronounced his name, and the donkey glared at her.

"He's right, I've read the files, I shouldn't have approached. Sorry Timaeus," said Ursula from her spot behind Fi.

He nodded regally and went back to nosing the grass.

"Shall we go?" Fi said brightly. Maybe today would be more interesting than she'd hoped.

Ursula nodded, eyeing the blue magic playing over Fi's fingertips as the tech witch shook her power away. She swallowed and led the way into town.

Chapter 11

At the café, Fi plonked the metal biscuit tin containing the scones on the counter and sank into an empty chair. Listening to Ursula exclaim about every little thing that reminded her of her childhood here in Omensford was exhausting.

If she liked it so much, why did she ever leave? Cressida grumbled from under Fi's chair.

Fi nodded. That was something they agreed on. At least the older witch had bumped into some friends in the street, so Fi could get a break from the constant twittering.

She took a deep breath and regretted it. The usual comforting coffee smell was tinged with a smoky floral odour of incense that clung to Fi's nostrils. She wondered how Steve could stand it with his ultra-sensitive werewolf nose.

Steve cracked open the tin and grinned. "Thanks, Fi, I need to get a regular order from you. How about a coffee?"

"And a bacon sandwich, please. Extra crispy with ketchup."

Cressida coughed.

"And an extra piece of charred bacon for Cressida."

"Coming right up." Steve turned to the elaborate coffee machine set up behind the counter, then span back round. "Actually, would you mind having a look? It's doing that spurting thing again, and you're the only one who can fix it."

He made a pleading face and Fi rolled her eyes before she got up to help. It just wasn't fair that werewolves were so good at making cute puppy dog eyes.

The machine purred as she approached. She tried it out and made a perfect black americano. "Seems to be working fine. Are you sure it's not just the normal noise of the steam valve releasing?"

"Try a cappuccino," Steve called from the kitchen.

Fi shook her head and packed a fresh sump of coffee granules.

"How's it going with the vampire?"

"I haven't seen him. He was already in bed when I arrived this morning, but he stinks. I've had to light some incense to cover the smell." That explained the overpowering floral scent that hung around the café.

"And he ordered some blood to the café. It gave me a fright when it turned up with the milk order. I tried to wake him, but he's dead to the world. It's in the fridge next to the juice! Can you believe it? Oh, and he left you a note asking about the fire at his place. Something about arson and the Anti Magic Alliance? They're not active round here, are they? Should I warn Glen?"

"No, I'm sure it's fine." The last thing she needed was an overprotective werewolf patrolling the streets.

Steve handed over a curling yellow post-it torn from the pad by the till. Fi read it and groaned. She hadn't made any progress finding out who had burned down his house. In fact, she hadn't even filed the report. Fi bit her lip, worrying about how the supervisor would take that.

"How lovely to see some old friends, and I love what the new Effie has done with this place..." Ursula trailed off as she caught sight of Fi behind the counter.

"Do you want a coffee?"

"Are you working here?" Ursula asked.

"Er, no, just checking the machine."

"The Magical Liaison Office has strict rules regarding second jobs."

"I'm just helping Steve out."

"Still..." Ursula took out a notebook and scribbled something down.

"I'm not getting paid, so it doesn't count as a second job...besides I'm a community agent, I've got to help out in the community."

Ursula frowned and looked confused. "I suppose." She jotted something else down. "And yes, a coffee sounds lovely. Cappuccino please."

Fi grinned. "Perfect." She handed over the drink she'd just made as Steve walked back with the bacon sandwich.

"It's running great, Steve."

"If you say so. Oh, hello ma'am, can I get you anything to eat? These scones are spectacular, I've been begging Fi to give me her secret recipe…"

Fi frantically made small gestures to get him to stop, and he trailed off in confusion.

"Yes, please." Ursula stretched her thin lips into a smile. "Fiona is clearly a woman of many talents."

"Er, I don't have a contract for this," Fi said, trying to salvage the situation.

"Not yet. I'll get something written up and I've recorded how much I owe you here, so I'll pay up at the end of the week."

"Really, Steve, there's no need." Fi gritted her teeth.

Ursula looked over the top of her winged glasses and made another note in her pink book. Super. At this rate, Fi would be kicked out of the Magical Liaison Office with less than two years' service.

"It's not–"

Ursula raised her pen to cut Fi off. "Really, there's no need to explain. I understand perfectly."

Fi opened her mouth to protest, but the bell above the door gave a quiet tinkle. Steve winced, his sensitive werewolf ears attuned to any sudden noise.

Agatha, Fi's sister, walked in with her daughter skipping at her side.

"Aunty Fi!"

"Bumble Bea! Great to see you." Fi rushed forward and lifted her niece off the floor in a tight hug as Agatha ordered two hot chocolates to go.

"Effie said your ex was in town," Agatha said without preamble. So much for confidence between witches. "Is this the return of Feely Fi-Li?"

Fi groaned at the old joke. Yes, their names were Fi and Li. Yes, it was an easy pun. But she hated it. It always reminded her of how much she loathed touchy feely stuff, especially with her ex. Fi shuddered just thinking about his cloying need and the way he always wanted to be in contact with her; a possessive hand on her shoulder or arm round her waist. Like she was something he could own.

Ursula saved her from an uncomfortable chat with her sister. "Oh, you must be Agatha! Nell's told me all about you."

Agatha shot Fi a questioning look.

"Agatha, this is Ursula. Ursula meet Agatha, my sister."

"I used to go to school with your mother."

"Really?" Agatha leaned forward, her eyes sparkling with interest. "I bet you could tell us all sorts of stories."

"Oh, yes, yes I could. I'm sure you already know about the trouble we got into with that gang of incubi…" Ursula let out a hearty laugh. "But we've got work to do. Chop chop Fiona."

Fi took a bite out of her bacon sandwich and grabbed her coat from the back of the chair. Cressida snapped at her ankles and Fi dropped the extra piece of crispy bacon down to her before she followed Ursula to the door.

Agatha gripped Fi's arm as Ursula stepped outside.

"Mum hardly ever talks about her schooldays. You have to get some gossip on her."

"She's here to supervise me, not share stories about her past."

"Fi." Agatha grabbed her sister's shoulders. "This could be our one chance to find out about Mum's past. You cannot waste this opportunity."

At least Agatha had moved on from the subject of her ex. "Fine. I'll do my best, OK?"

"Good. And let me know everything."

Fi nodded, even though she didn't understand her sister's need to know details about other people's lives. Sometimes it was hard to believe they were related; Agatha loved figuring out how people worked and taking care of them, whereas Fi was more interested in understanding how machines worked and solving problems.

Chapter 12

"Righto, where shall we start?"

"Er, what do you want to know?" Fi replied through a mouthful of sandwich. Steve had got the ratio of ketchup to bacon to bread perfect, and it was a slice of greasy piggy heaven.

"As we're in town, why don't you show me this shoe shop? That's your latest case, isn't it?"

Ursula was up to date. Fi had only pressed send on the report yesterday.

Fi nodded and led the way down the High Street to the *Well Heeled* shoe shop. They walked in and Fi pointed to the refilled display unit where the red shoes had been.

"Can I help you?" The shopkeeper, Madeline, bustled over, scenting a sale, before she recognised Fi. "Oh, it's you." Her gaze snapped down to Cressida. "No pets."

"She's my familiar."

Madeline narrowed her eyes and took in the half-eaten sandwich in Fi's hand. "No food in the shop."

Fi stuffed the rest of the bacony goodness into her mouth as the shopkeeper continued. "Any news on the case?"

"Nmfyem." Fi replied with her mouth full.

"Not yet," Ursula took over and smoothly showed her badge. "I wanted to get a look at the display." She bent forward and waggled her fingers over the shelves. "But it doesn't seem as though anything's amiss. We'll let you know if we find anything. Good day."

Fi followed as Ursula swept out of the shop.

"Always let them think you're in complete control of the situation. That's half the job."

Fi nodded. Maybe she should take notes. She trailed after the older witch, watching her caramel-coloured bob sway as she sashayed down the street. Fi felt the knot of tension in her body ease. The witch might be here to spy on her, but she had a wealth of experience she could pass on.

The last MLO training session had been cancelled due to an undisclosed incident at the training centre, and her magic was so volatile that she didn't like to practise too much on her own. Maybe she should treat this as an opportunity to learn.

Ursula stopped and turned to face Fi so abruptly that she almost slammed into the older witch. "Nothing of use about the case in there."

I could have told you that, Cressida said, unimpressed with the witch.

"So, what now?" asked Ursula.

Fi twisted a strand of hair that blew about her face and thought about what the senior agent would like to hear. "Er, well, there was a fire at a vampire house on Halloween. I haven't had time to get out there and have a look, but it could be a hate crime against a magical being."

"Righto. Lead on."

"We'll have to take a bus out there. I can't drive."

"Really? Seems like a disadvantage for an agent." Another note in that wretched book. "But, no matter. You're a witch, aren't you? Let's take a broomstick."

Chapter 13

Fi stared at the contents of the broom cupboard under the stairs and selected her own vacuum cleaner and her mum's broomstick. Her mother had said that 'of course she didn't mind her friend using her broomstick, as long as she didn't break it', with an edge to her voice that suggested Ursula had broken something important of hers before.

Ursula accepted the broom with a bright smile, but her face creased into confused lines as she took in the X-5000 with its purple and silver trim. "You ride a hoover?"

"Technically it's a Suxor, but yes. It works better with my magic, being electric."

"Interesting. And do you ride other white goods?"

"Er, no."

"And is your familiar coming?"

No, she is not. She is staying here in the warm.

"No," Fi said, eyeing Cressida, "she doesn't like the cold and, for some reason, is referring to herself in the third person."

Cressida hissed in response.

Ursula made a note in her book – Fi hated that fluffy notebook – and they headed outside. Fi caught her mum's pale face staring out of one of the upstairs windows as she programmed the address into her phone.

"Er, is there something going on with you and Mum?"

"Hmmm? Oh, no, she's just never forgiven me for breaking her broom when we were at school, but I had to use something to distract the tarfangtula while I conjured up enough ice to freeze its legs."

"O…K…"

Ursula turned and waved to Nell, who disappeared away from the window. Fi had trouble imagining the squat witch taking on a huge tarfangtula; the enormous spider like monsters weren't known for their kind natures and squads of Magical Liaison Office agents were called in whenever one was spotted. Clearly, Agent Fortescue wasn't just a bureaucrat.

Fi allowed some of her power to trickle into the X-5000 and kicked off into the air to the sound of the vacuum's purr. Flight made talking impossible, and Fi's mind whirled with worries.

How bad was it that she helped out in the café? And why was it a problem that her mode of transport was a vacuum cleaner? This one was cordless and as easy to stow away as a broom.

She tilted the X-5000 down and to the right, angling to avoid a flock of birds spiralling above the town. One of them turned into her and collided with her arm in a flurry of squawking feathers. It recovered and joined its flock, still chattering.

After a short, cold flight, Fi signalled to the other witch and started her descent. From up here, the blackened building was obvious, and the scent of smoke lingered in the air. Fi landed in the back garden, self-conscious about stumbling in front of the public, and stared up at the house, taking in the charred brick and shattered glass.

"This was arson, you say?"

Fi nodded, "That's what Valentine said."

She approached the house. The blaze had been fierce if the blackened bricks showed the height of the flames surging from the window. She shuddered. If the vampire had been sleeping in the basement during the day, would he have made it out?

"Best not to go in. You never know with fires." Ursula reached out to touch the bricks, curling a lip at the burned building.

Fi turned, anger burning bright in her chest. This wasn't an accident. This was an attack against a vampire. And the cowards had expected him to be asleep and helpless. It was attempted murder.

Her power crawled under her skin. Cowards like the Anti Magic Alliance. They were the worst, and if she found out that they had anything to do with this, she'd take their forum down for starters before making the internet a hostile place for all the members.

She caught Ursula regarding her with a thoughtful look and forced her power down. The last thing she needed was to lose control in front of her supervisor.

A bright red smudge under a bush caught her eye, and she walked over. A hat. She held it up to Ursula, who nodded and retrieved an evidence bag from her purse. Fi raised an eyebrow. Maybe she should start carrying evidence bags in her coat.

"Should we give it to the police?"

Ursula paused for a moment, waving her hand over the hat. "Absolutely. I can't sense any magic, so might as well hand it over. Do you have the fire report?"

"Er, no. Not yet. I need to request it."

The older agent span in a circle. "Can't sense any other magic here. No point staying."

"You can sense magic too?"

Could everyone apart from her sense magic?

"Of course, all magic users can tell if magic is in use or has been used recently."

Fi bit her lip. "Can you…can you teach me?"

Ursula blinked. "You mean you can't… Right. Yes. Of course. I wanted to see you train, anyway."

"Train?"

"Yes. I've read your training reports and I'd like to see your magic in action."

"OK…" Fi's shoulders tensed and the knot of worry was back in her stomach like a lead balloon. Her power was not something she liked to use. Even though she had better control now than in the past, it was still unpredictable. At least she could make sure that they were away from other people. "Why don't we go back to Mum's, and we can practise in the garden?"

Fi was fairly confident that her mum had got a magical barrier around their house, and it would be safest there. Ursula nodded her agreement, and they set off back to the Bed & Breakfast.

Chapter 14

As they flew into the garden, Ursula mistimed the wind speed and collided with a branch. The broomstick kept going, leaving her dangling from the tree, hugging the branch as her legs kicked under her. It would have been funny if Timaeus hadn't circled underneath, his red eyes glinting as he snapped at the witch's wellies.

Fi coaxed him away with some apples and the promise of a carrot a split second before the branch gave way under Ursula's weight. The witch plummeted to the ground, shooting out a flurry of freezing magic from her fingers and she slid to the grass on an icy luge. Both witches scurried away from the demon, and Ursula brushed herself down as the ice melted away.

"Let's put the broom…and vacuum away and get training. Where did that broomstick go?"

They scanned the garden, and Fi pointed. There, underneath one of the shutters that lined the house's windows, was a shattered broom.

Ursula bent over and gathered up the pieces just as Nell exited the house.

"You're back. What's that?"

The agent shifted in her wellies. "I am so sorry, Nelly. It was an accident."

"Is that…my broom?"

"I'll buy you a new one."

"Yes."

"It really wasn't her fault, Mum–"

Nell held up her hand. "I don't have time. The St Columba's branch of the WWWI needs my help with a jam disaster. I was going to use my broomstick, but I can see that's not going to happen, so I'll have to call your sister for a lift. I'll see you later." With that, she turned and headed back inside as Cressida hopped down the steps.

Fi turned her eyes upwards. It would never occur to her mother to take the bus, instead, her sister would have to deal with the fallout from Ursula's mistimed landing.

What's happened here?

"Mum's in a mood because Ursula broke her broom."

Seems a bit irresponsible for a senior witch, Cressida said as she perched on the low wooden bench with a hiss at Timaeus as he wandered too close.

"Righto, no time like the present." Ursula rubbed her hands together. "Let's start with some simple exercises. Where are your targets?"

"Er…"

"You don't have training targets?"

"No…"

"No problem." She made a complicated movement with her hands and blocks of ice shuddered up through the grass. Ursula smiled. "Lovely. Now, I want you to send some bolts of your magic at each of these targets so I can get an idea of your power. Don't worry, this is just a bit of fun. We'll build up to something more challenging."

Fi's body tensed even further. She didn't like the glint in the older agent's eye. Fi only used her magic when she absolutely had to, and it went against her entire experience to use it in front of others 'for fun'.

Relax, this will be good for you.

"Who's side are you on?" Fi mumbled.

Yours. Like always, came Cressida's reply.

She took a deep breath and called on her magic, allowing it to bubble to the surface instead of forcing it down. Fi focused and drew her electricity to one hand, forming a blueish white ball. She aimed at the closest target.

"Stand back."

Ursula dutifully took two steps back until she was behind Fi. The tech witch inhaled again, and blasted the ball of electricity at one of the lumps of ice. It soared over the white ice and hit one of her mother's fruit trees, scorching the thick trunk.

Fi winced. "Sorry, I…"

"You weren't concentrating."

"What?"

You mean, 'pardon'.

"You were worrying about hurting me or that donkey, and with power like yours, you need to focus." Ursula stepped up beside Fi, her hand coated with her own brand of elemental magic. With a flick of her wrist, the magic twisted away, leaping from ice crystal to ice crystal with a flourish. Ursula cut off the magic with a finger click and faced Fi.

"You're powerful, that much is clear, and I wouldn't expect anything less of Nell's daughter, but if you can't accept your magic then you can't bring it under control and that's a risk I'm not willing to take in one of our agents."

"Of course I accept my magic. It's part of me, isn't it?"

Cressida gave her a look, and Fi couldn't meet her emerald eyes. So what if she still wasn't comfortable with her unique brand of magical power? She was better than she had been, and that would have to be enough.

"You can't fool me, girly. You might resign yourself to it, but you haven't accepted it, or you'd be able to do what I just did."

Fi clamped her lips together and gathered her power back to her hands. She forced her magic out and this time it hit one of the targets with a crack and split the mini glacier into two pieces. Fi pulled a face.

"You've got the power, but no finesse. This time, I want you to concentrate on getting your power to dance around one of the bergs without destroying it."

From across the enormous garden, Timaeus brayed with derision. Fi narrowed her eyes at the demonic donkey, then tried sending a wave of electricity across the grass. It crashed into the icy blocks with a static crackle before fading away. She shook her fingers, annoyed with herself and unable to keep still.

"This isn't working."

Ursula tapped one thick finger to her face and sucked her lip as she contemplated. "Ask your familiar to help you."

"What?"

Pardon.

"You have a bond, yes." It wasn't a question. "Use the bond to help channel your magic."

"What?"

Ursula levelled a stare at Fi, peering over the rims of her oversized pink glasses. "Are you telling me that you've been bonded for over a year, and you haven't shared magic with your familiar?"

"Er, yes?"

"And your familiar has been bonded before, hasn't she? Didn't she tell you what to do?"

Fi looked down at the small wyrm. "No, she never mentioned it."

Cressida shifted on her clawed feet before racing inside. Fi sighed. "I think that's enough practice for now. I'd better go talk to my familiar."

Chapter 15

Cressida fled inside and ran upstairs to her witch's room. She'd been found out. A familiar bond was supposed to be sacred, an expression of trust between animal and magic user, and she'd kept part of their bond a secret.

Footsteps pounded up the stairs, and she scrabbled under the bed, retreating to the farthest corner behind discarded socks and an old textbook. Cressida curled up into the smallest ball she could and shut her eyes, panting as her emotions threatened to overwhelm her. She had to get herself under control.

"Cressida?"

The wyrm ignored Fiona's call. How could she face her witch now that Fiona knew she had betrayed her?

Feet paced, then stopped in the narrow space of the bedroom that Cressida could see.

"Cress, are you in here?"

Her tongue flicked out in annoyance. Why did the witch insist on shortening her name?

A pale face appeared, and Cressida held back the burst of flames she wanted to let loose. It wasn't fair. Just as her and Fiona were getting to some sort of agreement, it was ruined and her witch would abandon her and she'd be alone again, with only the pain of an empty bond. And it was all her fault. That was the worst part of this.

She should have been honest about the depths of the bond from the start, but losing Goody, her previous witch, had wrenched her heart in two and then to be immediately bonded to a strange witch with different powers, who didn't want her, had deepened her grief. The pain had dulled over time, but she still felt the hole in her life where Goody had been, and it was so raw now, a year on, almost to the day.

A whimper escaped, and she snapped at the hand Fiona offered her, lashing out against her witch. Another mark against her. She was the worst familiar ever to be bonded with a witch.

Fiona whipped her arm back and Cressida heard the creak of springs as she sat on the bed. Shoes came into view again, swinging this time as Fiona kicked her feet. That witch could never keep still. So much energy and magic bubbled inside her.

"So, do you want to tell me what that was about?"

The wyrm kept silent. A familiar was meant to aid her witch and the bond should be a warm expression of love and trust, and she'd ruined it. Cressida focused on a smear of mud on the tread of the trainer as it swung back and forth. She heard her witch slump further on the bed, so undignified but so Fiona; Goody always sat up bolt upright and with purpose, but Fiona fidgeted and fussed wherever she was.

Something akin to a smile curved on Cressida's lips. She had never thought that she would be fond of Fiona's quirks. A long silence spun between them. Through the familiar bond, she could feel her witch's frustration and confusion.

"I'm not going to force you to talk, and I don't pretend to know what's going on or what you're feeling, but I'm here. Whenever you're ready. I'm not going anywhere."

She wouldn't either. Cressida softened. Fiona might pretend not to understand feelings or people, but she was there when it counted, and she'd took Cressida in and even gone on a course to be a better wyrm handler.

The wyrm screwed her eyes shut. Just last night, she had berated Fiona for running away, and here she was; hiding under a bed. Maybe they were more alike than she thought. Cressida opened her eyes and resolve filled her reptilian face. She may be small, but she'd never been a coward.

Cressida inched forward. Perhaps it was time she shared more with her witch. Her head nudged Fiona's foot as she crawled out from her hiding place, and she jumped up onto the bed and laid her head on her witch's lap.

Fiona scratched the wyrm's neck but said nothing. She didn't even have her phone in her hand, which told Cressida more than words that her witch really cared for her.

Cressida stayed silent for several minutes, unsure how to start, allowing her witch to provide comfort.

I'm sorry. I've been a bad familiar.

"What are you talking about? You're the best familiar."

No, I've kept things from you when I could have helped.

"Stop being so hard on yourself. You saved my life when those bees attacked and when Adriana tried to kill me."

Cressida nuzzled into Fiona's hand, needing a stronger connection with her witch. *No,* she shook her head, *I've held back from this bond. I just…I didn't…I was scared.*

"Hey, hearing you speak in my head for the first time was freaky for me too. But, I'll never hurt you."

You might leave me, though. Cressida pulled her head away and buried it in the cartoon covered duvet. That was the crux of it. If she got close to a new witch, she opened herself up to pain if Fi left her. If her witch died. Again.

There was a long pause, then a tentative hand stroked her scales.

"Cress, I mean, Cressida, I know we started off on the wrong foot, but I won't leave you. Not deliberately."

Do you mean that?

"Of course, who else is going to tell me off when I shorten someone's name or say what instead of pardon?"

The wyrm turned her emerald eyes on her witch.

"I know losing Goody Winships was a big change for you, and I'm sorry I never talk about her, but I didn't want to upset you, and I didn't really know her, except that Mum didn't get on with her, and I guess it was just easier to pretend everything's alright. But it isn't, and I'm sorry."

She was a good witch, you know.

"Tell me about her."

Chapter 16

Cressida began talking, letting loose the floodgates of feelings and memories she had bottled up for a year.

She couldn't stop.

She spoke about the day they had met at a Witches', Wizards' and Warlocks' Institute trip to the Dragon Ranch and formed an instant familiar bond, how Goody sent her out to spy on other magic users in Magewell, how Cressida learned to read by poring over spell books that the witch had used to enhance her magic.

She shared memories of being quietly curled up by the fire while Goody read, and WWWI meetings fraught with tension and power struggles. And finally, she spoke about the familiar bond, and how it could help Goody channel her magic and create more finesse and power than she'd had before.

"She was very special to you, and I'm sorry I didn't realise how badly you were hurting." Fi pulled Cressida into a warm cuddle.

Sorry I didn't tell you about the familiar bond and how it could help with magic. I knew you were struggling with control, and I kept silent instead of nurturing our bond. Somehow, it felt that deepening our bond into magic use would betray my connection with Goody. I've been so stupid.

"It's OK, Cressida. I don't blame you. I'm not the easiest person to get along with. You can help me now." Cressida regarded her with narrowed eyes. "I mean, if you want…no pressure…"

How are you so accepting of faults in others, but you judge yourself for every tiny failing?

"Killing someone isn't exactly a tiny failing."

Cressida snorted. *If you're talking about Margaret, she was trying to kill you and Agatha. What else were you meant to do?*

"Find another way," Fiona grumbled.

Cressida tsked and flicked out her pink tongue in annoyance at her witch. *There isn't always a good choice, you know. This is real life, not some fairy tale.*

"Maybe this familiar bond could help with training?"

Typical Fiona, deflecting from uncomfortable truths. But she couldn't push her witch away. The wyrm inhaled and let out a breath of hot air. It was time to ally herself properly with her magic user.

To use the familiar bond for your magic, you need to reach inside and access my power as well as your own.

"Wyrms have magic?"

I don't know about other wyrms, but familiars can help their witches. Have you had any sense of my emotions through the bond?

Fiona's brow creased as she thought. "I'm not sure. Maybe. There have been a couple of times where I've felt weird, like I was experiencing emotions that weren't my own…"

That could be it. So, instead of ignoring that, focus on it. What am I feeling now? Cressida concentrated on her positive feelings of contentment and acceptance of the bond instead of her feelings of failure.

Fiona closed her eyes and rested a hand on the wyrm's golden scales. "I can feel…that you're happy?"

Yes, good.

"…And, oh Cressida, you're still hurting. There's so much grief."

Cressida swallowed. She hadn't wanted to pass those feelings to her witch. She was a strong wyrm, descended from a pedigree line and familiar to the most powerful witch in the Cotswolds; she should have better control.

You've got it. So now that you can feel that bond, you can use that to help channel your magic.

"How?"

Try using your power but use our connection to ground it.

Fiona's fingers sparked as she drew her electrical magic to her palm. Cressida could sense her concentration and fear of losing control through the bond with a depth she had never felt before. Sympathy for the young witch flooded her. This poor woman lived with so much fear and self-doubt.

Trust yourself and use our bond.

Fiona's magic flared and crackled up from her hand in a tower of blue light that seared a black mark on the ceiling. The house creaked and groaned and jolted the floor hard enough to knock both witch and familiar from the bed. Cressida hissed her displeasure as she panted on the floor, the sudden tug of magic sapping her strength. Fiona winced and apologised to the semi-sentient house, patting the floor affectionately before turning to Cressida.

"What was that?"

That's what happens when you use the bond to enhance your magic. The bond uses both of our strength to amplify your power. But you can siphon some of your power to me for more controlled magic. Shall we try?

The house shuddered, and the door swung open, slamming against the wall. Unsubtle as only a pile of bricks could be.

"I think that's enough magic use inside." Fiona rubbed her brow. "And I could use a coffee."

Chapter 17

The two companions headed downstairs and refuelled. Fi made herself a black coffee and sweetened it with two sugars while she raided the biscuit tin and dug out a chunk of premium Welsh coal for her familiar.

"Are you ready to head back outside?" Fi asked the small wyrm around a mouth full of crumbly shortbread.

Now's as good a time as any.

Fi offered Cressida her arm, and the wyrm hopped up onto the witch's shoulder, a show of togetherness as they stepped out of the house. The door swung shut behind them and Fi screwed up her face as she heard the lock click into place. The house didn't have any confidence in her magic.

Ursula sat on the wooden bench, a steaming cup of something in her hand, and…was she chatting with Timaeus? Fi strode over and slouched into the space next to the MLO agent.

"So, the demon realm really is frozen over? Oh, hello Fi, ready to do some more training."

"Yep, we're good, right Cressida?"

Right.

"Righto, let's get back to work. Lovely to talk with you, Timaeus." The donkey grunted and stalked off to nose for apples in the grass. "Right then, show me what you've got."

Fi closed her eyes and felt inside her heart for the connection with Cressida. She found a slight tugging sensation and a feeling of pride coupled with trepidation. Fi pulled her magic to her hands and blasted a bolt of lightning at a block of ice. After three seconds, she cut off her power and forced it back down, shaking her hands at the enormous shock of electricity that had passed through them.

Ursula regarded the shards that scattered the lawn and quirked an eyebrow. "Thought you must be powerful, but let's try a bit of finesse now, shall we? See if you can make a shape out of your magic."

Fi frowned. "What do you mean?"

Ursula tipped her palm up, and a silvery glow coated her hand. She moved her fingers, and the magic formed the shape of a flower. "Magic is available to all magical beings. Some are limited, such as werewolves who have physical abilities but no way to manipulate magic, but all classes of witches, including wizards and warlocks, can shape magic to our needs. Our only limitation is the strength and source of our power. As you can see, I'm a weather witch, and my power is linked to the natural world, much like your mother's. I can use it to affect the environment, although water and ice are my preferred elements."

"Like forcing ice up from underground."

"Precisely. But this is the elemental form of my magic, and I can will it to form any shape I imagine. It's exactly what you do when you create the balls of electricity. They are spherical because you imagine them to be so."

Fi's brow crinkled. Her magic just formed a ball, it was hard to believe she had any control over it. Her scalp prickled as her hair lifted with the static from using her magic.

"The more powerful you are, the harder it is to form delicate shapes, so why don't you start with something simple but different to your natural preference, like a cube instead of a ball? Go on, try it." Ursula clenched her hand into a fist and the glowing flower disappeared.

Fi breathed in and out.

You can do this.

She smiled at her familiar's encouragement and let her magic flow back into her hand. It gathered in a familiar blue ball of electrical energy, and she squinted and bit her lip as she willed it to form a cube. One side of the ball squashed in slightly, as if it had collapsed, before it bounced back out into a sphere with a shower of sparks.

"Good. Now you can use your familiar to help you. You can share strength and power through the bond you have. Let Cressida help you shape the magic."

"OK Cressida, you're up." Fi searched for that strange tugging sensation in her chest.

You're fighting me. You have to open up to the bond as well.

Fi's face scrunched as she concentrated on letting Cressida in. It was an odd, uncomfortable prickly feeling as the wyrm's consciousness melded with hers and then it was freeing as the burden of her discomfort and worries about never fitting in and hurting someone with her magic ebbed through her familiar, who she knew, deep inside her core, would always accept her as she was.

"Wow," she breathed. It was so intimate, like a joining of souls, and so…right. No wonder Cressida had been scared about sharing this with her. And then, with a sliding click, they synced together, and Fi knew in her soul that she could share her magic with Cressida and not hurt her.

"I'm going to pass you some of my magic."

Yes.

Instead of tamping down her power and forcing it deep within her, Fi channelled it through the familiar bond to the small wyrm. Cressida's eyes glowed blue as she accepted the electrical magic. The ball in Fi's hand dimmed and shrank down.

"Good, now don't give away too much. You still want something to shape, remember?" Ursula watched on, her eyes glinting behind their pink frames.

Fi nodded and her mouth twisted as she forced the sphere into a cube. Her eyes widened, surprised at her own skill. "Look! I've done it!"

Well done, Fiona. I knew you could do it.

"Lovely. Now let's get on to the hard work."

Chapter 18

After over an hour of shaping electricity into shapes, Ursula gestured that they could take a break.

"Now you've got more control over your magic, we can start thinking about more subtle uses for it."

"Like sensing enchantments?"

"Exactly." Ursula pulled one of the red shoes out of her bag. "Here. To sense magic, you need to be in close proximity to it, although the more powerful you are, the further away you can be."

Fi waved her hand over the shoe. She felt nothing. "What am I meant to feel?"

"When you're starting out, you have to concentrate, not wave your arms aimlessly. I don't know what it feels like for you, but for me it's a pressure behind my eyes. Try again."

Fi moved her hand slowly, closing her eyes and reaching out with her senses. Still nothing. All she felt was her own magic bubbling within her. "It's no good!"

Ursula pursed her lips. "Try using your familiar bond. You have a lot of power; it might be clouding your ability to sense magic that isn't yours."

That made some sort of sense. Fi placed one hand on the wyrm in her lap and kept the other over the scuffed shoe. She closed her eyes and reached first for the tug of the familiar bond, feeling Cressida's soothing calmness dampen her crackling magic. Then she concentrated on the hand over the shoe.

"Nothing."

"Breathe. Clear your mind. What meditation do you practise?"

"Er…"

Ursula sighed. "Like this." She demonstrated taking a deep breath in and out.

Fi copied her, fighting the urge to roll her eyes. Everyone knew how to breathe.

She tried again. Was that uncomfortable prickle the feel of an enchantment?

"I don't know, I might have felt something…"

"Maybe it's too early to sense enchantments. It's easier to feel unfamiliar magic when it's being cast. Here, try to sense my magic." Ursula gathered her power and formed a tiny rain cloud that she controlled by waving her hand to make it move around the garden in lazy circles.

Fi reached into herself and found the strange pull of the bond again. Cressida curled tighter against her neck, pressing her warm scales against Fi's skin. The tech witch reached up with one hand and stroked the small wyrm while she turned her other palm in Ursula's direction. She forced down her magic, but instead of dampening it within her, she shared it with her familiar, allowing Cressida to soothe her power.

A rush of strange magic brushed her fingertips. She closed her eyes and her brow puckered as she concentrated. There. She opened her eyes. A prickle of unfamiliar magic played underneath her hand and made her skin crawl. It felt like a stiff winter's breeze with a strange sensation of cool rain.

"I felt something." She shook out her hand. "Ugh, that was weird."

Ursula had a small smile on her lips. "That uncomfortable feeling is from magic that isn't like yours. As you get used to sensing other magic, you'll be able to identify the type of magic and if you become really adept, you'll be able to identify who cast it, like a signature. It's easiest to practise with other magic users you know well, like your family."

Fi rubbed her hands together. She couldn't wait to try it out and see what Aggy's magic felt like, and her mum's, and Mort's. For the first time in a long time, Fi was excited about her power instead of afraid of it.

Chapter 19

Fi practised until it was dark, using a combination of meditation breathing and the newly discovered familiar bond. She got better at sensing Ursula's magic, although she still couldn't feel anything more than a prickle when she tried to sense the enchanted shoe. She tried not to get too disappointed, but it was hard to feel like she was making progress when she couldn't trust if the wisp of unfamiliar magic was genuine or pins and needles in her palm.

When it came to using her power, however, Fi found that by using the familiar bond, she could make her magic into almost any shape, although a ball was still her default manifestation.

With Ursula's encouragement, she used less and less power, stretching her magic to create more refined forms and, while she struggled with natural illusions like flowers, she could accurately recreate a motherboard from the first computer she'd built. It hovered over her hand in a shimmer of blues and whites, rotating slightly as she studied it from all angles.

Once she was happy that all the connections were right, she focused, and the magic motherboard lifted from her hand and twirled around her head. Fi smiled. She was in control of her magic after so long fearing that it could hurt her loved ones, and maybe the familiar bond could make sure that wouldn't be an issue again.

She wanted to shout it from the sky, an immense weight lifting from her chest. Her mother would be proud, and Mort…Fi could imagine his lopsided smile when she showed him the motherboard. She bit her lip. Maybe he wouldn't be excited over a circuit, but she could make something else.

"Not exactly what I expected, but it's progress for certain. I'll make a note in my report. You really should have had more training; I don't know what the Office was thinking, allowing you into the field without proper control. No wonder we've had a complaint about you."

Fi frowned, and the illusion flickered out as Ursula's words distracted her. She hadn't lost control since she'd worked for the Magical Liaison Office.

She'd known what she was doing, even if she hadn't been confident about her power. She'd blasted Adriana after the evil witch had killed Effie and attacked her and Cressida and she'd saved the world from a demon attack and protected a sentient pumpkin from being killed.

Not bad for a year in the role.

"I haven't had a complaint about my magic."

Ursula peered over her spectacles at her book. "Undue force it says here."

Fi racked her brains. There was only one person she had hurt in her investigations, a vampire that she had stopped from fleeing.

Surely Valentine didn't hold that against her? He healed fast, and she'd had to do something to counter his supernatural speed. She opened her mouth, but a cry from near the gate flooded ice down her neck.

"Fiona! Are you ready?"

She had forgotten about her meal with her ex. Fi smoothed down her clothes out of habit and patted her hair, now frizzed into a static halo around her head after using so much magic. Now she had no time to get ready, not that she planned to dress up, but it would have been nice to shower and tame her hair before seeing Li for the first time since he'd walked out of the door and exited her life.

Fi swore, then apologised to Ursula. "Sorry, but I completely forgot – got to go – meeting someone for dinner."

Do you want me to come with you? Cressida eyed the man waiting politely at the end of the garden.

Fi gave it a microsecond of consideration. Probably not a good idea to take along a wyrm who openly disliked her ex. She'd be too eager to teach him a lesson.

Fi could feel the waves of anger roiling off her familiar through the new closeness of their bond.

"Thanks Cressida, but I think I'd better go alone. See you later."

Chapter 20

Fi allowed Li to embrace her in a hug at the gate, but she stayed stiff, feeling smothered by his instant show of affection. He pulled away.

"Love what you've done with your hair."

Fi compulsively patted at her frizzy white hair, trying to smooth it down, but it remained fluffy and uncontrollable after using her magic all afternoon and the best she could do was to pull it into a tight ponytail. Li smiled and gestured to the car.

"After you, my little witch."

Fi stiffened her spine at his old endearment for her. She wasn't his. Not anymore. Had he always been this condescending?

She led the way to the road, still fiddling with her long hair. He opened the car door for her, and she sank into the white leather seat. He shut the door firmly behind her and Fi fought the rising panic that bubbled in her chest. She should never have agreed to meet him. Her fists clenched into tight balls.

She felt trapped. Why couldn't he just get it over with and say whatever he wanted to say?

He took his time getting into the car and buckling his seatbelt. Annoyance helped to thaw some of the embarrassment and awkwardness that trapped her limbs.

"Can we have some music on?"

He gave her a breezy smile. "Now Fi, you know I don't like music when I drive. I like to hear the engine." He revved the car to prove his point and Fi stared out of the window. Of course, he wouldn't want her to feel at ease. He always put himself first. Why would that change? At least they weren't going far, only to Sorella's.

He found a parking space not far from the Italian restaurant and hopped out. Fi rushed to open her door before he did it for her, not wanting his forced chivalry. When he held his arm out to her, she gave him a look and headed for the restaurant by herself.

Li laughed. "Always so independent, aren't you?" He darted ahead and opened the door for her. Fi ground out a thank you and stepped into the warm eatery. He followed behind, placing one hand on her arm to steer her.

"I have a reservation for two, under Li Yeoh."

"Of course, Mr Yeoh, let me show you to your table."

The server showed them to a table towards the back, bathed in soft candlelight. Of course, Li had booked the table in a cosy, romantic corner. The one they'd joked was their 'usual' when they used to come here as a couple. He was a creature of habit. Or of control. Fi shifted as she sat down. She should have known better than to agree to somewhere that had so many memories for them.

Fi glared at him as he studied the menu. Why was he here anyway? Back in her town and her life. Why couldn't he stay away?

She took a sip of the water the server had left them and blurted out the question. "Why are you here, Li?"

He laughed again. "Straight to the point, aren't you? Let's at least wait until we've got some food in front of us."

Fi pursed her lips and studied her menu, even though she knew exactly what she was going to choose; pepperoni pizza.

The server returned, hovering at their table. He looked to Li first. "Can I take your drinks order?"

"A bottle of the house red, please." Li ordered smoothly, without even glancing at Fi.

"That's a lot of wine for you to drink," she said from behind the menu,

He laughed again, a sound that grated against her nerves. "Oh Fi, you're so funny, of course we'll share a bottle."

Her magic bubbled under her skin as she narrowed her eyes at her ex. Typical Li, always thinking he knew best. Where did he get off ordering for her? This time, she wouldn't sit here sipping at wine that she didn't even like.

"Actually, I'll have a diet coke, thanks."

Li raised a black eyebrow. "OK, I guess I'll have a large glass of the red."

The waiter looked between them, uncomfortable at the tension that built at their table. He jotted down their order. "I'll be right back."

"I'm ready to order food now, too," Fi said, keeping her eyes on Li, "pepperoni pizza, please."

"So decisive today. I'll have the linguini with extra prawns."

They sat in silence until the server returned with their drinks. Fi sipped hers, enjoying the tang of the fizzy cola as it hit her tongue.

Li steepled his fingers, and Fi eyed him over the rim of the glass. Maybe they could finally get to whatever he had to say, then she could run out of there.

"So, how are you?"

She swallowed. That was it. Well, she could be polite. "Fine, and you?"

"Good. Great."

"And we couldn't have had that conversation on the phone?"

He shook his head with a smile. "Fi, we haven't seen each other in years. Is it so hard to imagine that I just want to talk?"

Fi drummed her fingers on the table. Li stared at her hand sharply and Fi quelled her first instinct to stop. She tapped more deliberately, welcoming the knowledge that she was getting under his skin.

"Given how we split up, I'd say, yes, it is that hard to imagine."

Chapter 21

Li leaned back in his chair and took a sip of his own drink. "That's fair. We didn't exactly leave on the best terms."

Fi pretended to think. "If I remember, you said something like you couldn't live with a robot anymore, before storming out."

"Can you blame me? You preferred being on the computer to being in a genuine relationship."

"I needed my space."

"Then why did you agree to move in together?"

Fi took another drink. That was a good question. She hadn't thought about it at the time. They were going out, and that was one of the things you did when you'd been together for a few months. It was like levelling up or getting a relationship achievement. But she hadn't been all in.

Fi resented her ex for intruding on her personal space and not giving her the time away that she craved, and when he'd given her an ultimatum, she had chosen her computer over him.

"It seemed like the right thing to do."

Li sighed and Fi got the impression she had said both the right and the wrong thing, but then his smile was back.

"We were both young and stupid. We didn't know what we wanted. But now we're more adult, can we at least have a conversation?"

It was a reasonable request, and it irked Fi that he was the one to suggest it. "Sure." She sounded like a sullen teenager. "I mean, of course, what did you want to talk about?"

"I hear you've moved back in with your mother…"

Fi's hands clenched into fists. "Are you spying on me?"

"No! I still have friends in the village, you know, someone mentioned it. Come on, I thought we were going to be civil."

Fi huffed out a sigh. This meal was a bad idea, and Li wound her up without even trying. It was annoying that he still had that much sway over her emotions, but apparently, he did. "I am back home. For now. And I've got a new job, in the Magical Liaison Office. Been there for over a year."

"Good for you, that's got to be the longest job you've had, hasn't it? But I'm surprised you left your beloved computers behind. You were so obsessed with your IT jobs when we were together."

Fi shifted in her seat as she fought back the urge to tell him that his overbearing need for affection was one of the reasons that she worked long hours back then. "And you?"

"Yes, still at the bank. Got a couple of promotions, actually. I'm doing pretty well, if I do say so myself. And your love life?"

Fi choked on her cola, feeling the bubbles fizz up her nostrils, and she grabbed a napkin as their food order arrived. She mopped at her mouth, annoyed that her cheeks turned red as Li sat there waiting.

"There is someone," she said before stuffing a slice of pizza into her mouth.

"Good, I'm glad you've found someone. A fellow IT nerd?"

"A doctor."

"Oh, well, good for you. I'm engaged, do you want to see the ring?"

No. "Yes."

He pulled out his phone – a flashy customised version of the latest Apple model – and brought up a photo of him and an attractive woman with flawless skin, flashing a ring with a diamond so large it looked fake.

"I'm happy for you." Fi surprised herself, but it was true. He might try to rub it in her face, the life she could have had – if she were prepared to sacrifice part of herself to him – but she didn't care. She didn't want that life. And a weight lifted off her shoulders when he announced his engagement. She didn't have to worry about Li trying to rekindle a relationship, and some of her nerves flitted away. Fi smiled.

"I knew you would be. Rhia's a model."

"Rhia?" Fi snorted. "Rhi-Li?"

He grinned, missing her pun. Fi took a drink to compose herself while he prattled on. "You might have seen her in the latest Vogue campaign…"

Fi nodded to be polite. As if she read Vogue. Now, if Rhia had been in Computer Weekly talking about the best value external hard drives, she might have recognised her.

"…and with my latest bonus and her career taking off, we're thinking of finding a place in the country, settling down. Naturally, we'll keep the London pad, but we wanted somewhere quaint and countrified…"

Fi nodded, finding it hard to picture Li living a quiet life in the country.

"…and I thought, why not choose somewhere that I already know, so we're thinking of moving to Omensford."

So that was why he was here. "Really? Out of the entire country, you choose here?"

"Of course, why not?" That laugh again. "But I wanted to check," his face turned serious, "that it wouldn't be too awkward. Seeing me around with my future wife in your hometown. I mean, it's not like we could avoid each other in this place."

Fi chewed her pizza and swallowed hard. The possibility of running into Li at unknown times grated at her, like he was trying to still have some control or impact on her life. But he was engaged, so he wouldn't deliberately move back because of her, would he?

What could she say that wouldn't make her sound like she still cared for him? Because the longer she sat here, the more she was sure that she did not have feelings for him, but that didn't mean she wanted him able to pop up in her life without notice.

Li kept going, talking over her silence as if she was simply an audience for his chatter, not giving her the space she needed to think.

"And I was wondering if I could buy your place, if you still have it. Just while we find somewhere else, get a feel for village life in a quaint little house. And Simon and Graham were such good neighbours."

Fi choked again. He wanted her to give up her house. The gall of this man. She had tenants. And responsibilities. And it was hers. Just knowing she could move back out of her mother's house meant she was happy to stay in a strange, paradoxical way. And he couldn't even get their neighbours' names right.

"Steve and Glen."

"Who?"

"The neighbours."

Li waved a hand. "Sure, they're great. So, what do you think?"

Fi's phone chirruped, making her jump. She glanced down, grateful for the interruption.

Fi – get here quick. Valentine's gone crazy.

She stood. "Sorry, Li. Emergency. Steve's in trouble. Got to go."

"You could at least have done better than making up a fake emergency to get out of the meal."

"It's not fake!"

He raised an eyebrow, and a knowing smile tilted his lips. Ugh, that superior know-it-all look that she'd seen so many times while they were going out and made her feel like she was a stupid girl. "Go on, run away. You're good at putting distance between us. I should have known we couldn't even have one conversation without your drama."

Fi's power crackled under her skin, and she gritted her teeth as she forced it down, refusing to allow him the satisfaction of seeing her lose control.

"You know what, Li? I don't owe you anything. I was curious about what you wanted to talk about tonight, but there is a genuine emergency and I have to go. Not everything is about you and your needs. Sometimes there are other people who need me." She flipped her ponytail over her shoulder.

"Goodbye Li, enjoy the rest of your evening and do whatever you want with your fiancée, I genuinely don't give a rat's bum, but I care about my friends and one of them is in trouble. I'll send you the money to cover my half."

She grinned as she walked away, leaving him bewildered at the table. That felt good, like a weight had lifted from her shoulders. When they were in a relationship, she'd always felt like she was walking on eggshells, never knowing what he would react badly to, and she had been sure it was her fault. But now she understood; just because she had different needs to him didn't mean it was all her problem, and Fi saw now how selfish he was, wanting all her attention, even when he was in another relationship.

Fi lifted her head and strode to the café with a newfound confidence. He wasn't part of her life anymore. But her friends were, and she would never run from them. She quickened her pace. She would run towards whoever needed her, and right now, Steve needed her help.

Chapter 22

Fi flung open the door to the café, panting hard even though she'd only run down the High Street from the Italian restaurant.

"Shut the door, for goodness' sake! No one else should have to see this." Steve jumped out from behind the counter and shoved Fi further into the shop. He glanced side to side out onto the street before shutting the door and leaning against it.

Fi stood with her mouth open as a very naked vampire strutted between the café tables.

"What the–?"

"He picked up a jacket that a customer had left and then stripped off."

Fi averted her eyes, but they kept sliding back to the pasty vampire. It was like watching a horror film; you knew you should look away, but you couldn't.

Valentine reached the back of the shop and struck a pose before he bent over to pick up a gemstone from the display. Fi grimaced.

"Don't you think this would go beautifully with my outfit?" Valentine asked.

"What outfit?"

He laughed. "Oh, you are silly. Look, I'm wearing the most wonderful robe. I don't think I'll ever take it off." He did another slow turn.

Something pinged in Fi's head. "Oh no, it's the Emperor's New Clothes."

"What?"

"The fairy tale where the emperor gets duped by some tailors into wearing nothing so they can steal his gold."

"I know the story, Fi, but what's that got to do with Valentine? He doesn't have any money, that's why he's living in the shop."

"Not the money, the enchantment. Where's the jacket?"

"Over there on the floor."

"And what did he do with it? Did he put it on?"

Steve's brow crinkled, and he shook his head. "He picked it up, said 'Finders, keepers.' and did one round of the shop with it over his shoulder, before he dropped it and started taking off his clothes. It was the worst strip tease I've ever seen. We still had customers!

Fi crouched next to the jacket. She reached out a hand.

"Don't pick it up! I can't risk you getting naked, too. Here, use these." Steve handed her the tongs he used for dolling out slices of cake.

Fi thanked him and held up the coat at arm's length. It was an ordinary leather jacket. She sniffed. "What's that smell?" Fi waved it towards Steve.

The werewolf inhaled and then snorted. "It's got a whiff of charity shop and perfume."

"Any people scent?"

He shook his head. "Sorry, but look, it's still got a label in it. Someone must have brought it today."

Fi frowned at the coat. Someone had enchanted the shoes and then this, but why? It didn't make any sense. Valentine had arrived a couple of days ago. Who would have a grudge against him…or want to see him naked? She risked a glance in his direction and looked away when she got an eyeful of him holding up jewels to his ears while pouting into a mirror, placed at an unfortunate angle that reflected more of him than she wanted to see.

The lines on her forehead deepened. "How can I see his reflection?"

Steve shrugged. "It's the modern mirrors. They're not silver backed."

Fi filed that away in useless trivia. "OK, the other enchantment stopped when we removed the shoes, but he's already not wearing the coat, so maybe it will wear off by itself?"

"I don't want him prancing around the shop like that. It's unsanitary. Besides, what if he's still strutting his stuff when the sun comes up?"

This was more deadly than she realised. If the spell forced him to keep modelling in the daytime, then prolonged exposure to sunlight would kill the vampire. She rubbed her forehead and huffed out a sigh. "Let's get him back to Mum's. Between Ursula and Mum, we've got a better chance of breaking this enchantment. Have you got anything we can put over him?"

Steve struggled out of his jumper, revealing a t-shirt that hugged his muscular chest like a second skin.

"You didn't bring a coat?"

"I get really warm."

Figured. She shrugged off her own tan trench coat. It would be a tight fit, but it would cover more of the vampire than the jumper.

"Here you are, your majesty, another robe to try on."

"Oh, I couldn't put that mangy thing on. It would damage these fine threads."

Fi rolled her eyes at his assessment of her best coat. "We wanted to take you, er, outside, to…show off your new clothes, but it would work so much better if there was a big reveal."

"If you're sure…"

"Very sure, and we've got a great modelling opportunity for you. Just come with us." Fi held out the coat and averted her eyes as Valentine put it on. He pouted again as Steve did up her jacket and pulled the belt tight. It hung to his mid-thigh, but at least it covered the important bits. Fi kept the other coat in the tongs, and they headed out into the night.

Chapter 23

After an incident outside the pub where Valentine decided to drop the coat, much to the amusement of the three old men who sat on their customary bench near the entryway and a gaggle of teenagers, who Fi wasn't sure were of an age to be imbibing alcohol, Fi and Steve took one of the vampire's arms each and frogmarched him to the Bed & Breakfast.

Timaeus snored in a series of demonic stutters, still standing up in one corner of the extensive garden, and Fi led the others to the back door. It opened as they stepped onto the small porch, and they shoved Valentine into the warm kitchen.

"I'd better go. Zadie can't sleep without her bedtime story," Steve said.

"You can't leave me with him!"

"Fi, is that you?" Fi's mum walked through the door that joined the kitchen to the rest of the house as Steve bolted outside.

Shut the door, it's cold in here. Cressida raised her head from her spot by the aga.

"Behold my finery." Valentine let the coat fall to the floor and thrust his hips at the older woman.

Nell pursed her lips and spoke directly to Fi. "What is the meaning of this? And cover yourself up young man, you'll catch your death."

"It's not his fault, Mum. There's some sort of enchantment on him." Fi placed the offending item of clothing on the table and retrieved her coat from the floor, trying to get it back on the vampire. He sped around the room at top speed, pausing to pose on everything from the table to the kitchen countertop.

Cressida hissed from her spot by the aga and darted under the table. *That's unsanitary.*

Nell raised an eyebrow. "You are wiping that down." She raised her hands and the large trailing plant that sat in the corner of the kitchen grew until it caught Valentine's wrist. He yanked hard, but the nature witch wrapped him with more of the leafy vines until he was incapacitated. With an extra twist, she made sure that the plant covered his unmentionables.

Nell selected a blue bottle from a cupboard and dropped a little of the liquid into the protesting vampire's mouth. His writhing stopped and his eyes closed as he fell into a peaceful slumber. Fi threw her coat over him for good measure. She'd have to get it dry cleaned anyway, it might as well do double duty and make sure his nude body didn't touch anything else.

"Now, what were you saying about an enchantment?"

Fi waved towards the jacket lying on the table as she dug around in the cupboard under the sink for some anti-bacterial spray. She'd be the first to admit she wasn't the tidiest of witches, but a naked man on the kitchen side, where they prepared food, made her insides squirm.

Nell moved her palms over the coat and nodded her head as Ursula entered the room.

"What's the commotion in here?" She stopped as she took in the snared vampire and the two witches. Ursula took a deep breath and Fi thought it was to her credit that she didn't draw magic to her hands at the unusual situation. "Do I need to write you up for kidnapping a magical being?"

Cressida hissed and arched her back at the threat to Fi.

"Don't be silly, Ursula. Fi rescued this vampire. Didn't you?"

Fi abandoned her cleaning and hurried over, nodding. "He touched that leather jacket and started stripping, so I brought him here. I think it's another enchantment, like the Emperor's New Clothes." Seeing their blank looks, she carried on, "He thinks he's wearing fancy clothes, but really, he's wearing nothing."

Nell tilted her head, considering. "Another fairy tale reference?"

"That's what I thought."

How can stories for children cause so much havoc? asked Cressida, slinking out from her spot under the table.

"Let's see what we've got here then…" Ursula said, reaching for the jacket.

"Don't touch that!"

Too late. Ursula grasped the leather between her fingers and her face became dreamy. She released the thick leather and began unbuttoning her woollen cardigan.

"Mum, the sleeping draught, quick!"

Nell snatched up the small blue bottle and gripped Ursula's chin with one bony hand as the other dripped two drops of the clear liquid into her mouth. Ursula smiled and fell backwards onto the hardwood floor.

Both witches and the wyrm stared at the two bodies on the kitchen floor. "We'd better get this sorted toot suite."

Fi nodded, warily picked up the jacket with the tongs and headed to the library.

Chapter 24

While her mum asked the library for books on the Emperor's New Clothes and enchanting clothing, Fi tried to sense the spell on the coat.

She waved her hand over the worn leather and reached inside for Cressida's stable presence through the familiar bond. That strange prickling sensation brushed against her palm with a tiny amount of pressure, a little stronger than the shoe, but it could still be her mind playing tricks on her. As her friend, Liv, the sleep therapist, would say, the mind is a powerful thing, it can make people believe anything.

"Can you sense the enchantment?" she asked her mum.

Her mother ran a hand lightly above the jacket, careful not to touch the faded leather surface. "I think it's the same magic user, but the enchantment has faded. Two uses must have almost used it up."

Fi pursed her lips. Nell was a powerful witch, almost a sorcerer, but she didn't have a familiar to help her. How could she sense something so subtle?

With a sigh, Fi gave up on the jacket and searched the internet with her phone while her mother went back to the books. There was nothing helpful; a few websites on how to hex clothes to make them itchy or cause rashes, but nothing about getting people to remove clothes.

"Whoever is doing this is powerful," Nell said as she put down another book in the pile and rubbed her eyes. "To enchant something so it has an effect without contact is difficult."

Omensford has more than its fair share of powerful magic users, Cressida commented from her spot next to Fi on the sofa.

Fi nodded; her mum's observation didn't narrow the suspect pool. With its protected magical status, Omensford drew magic users like flies to honey or like witches to tea and cake.

"All I can think is we need some way to shock them out of the enchantment…" Nell said an hour later, closing another book with a snap. Fi gave her a puzzled look and her mum continued, "In the story, when the emperor is told that he's naked, the spell breaks and he covers up."

"So, we just tell Valentine that he's not wearing clothes?"

"Have you got any better ideas?"

Fi didn't. "Alright, it's worth a try."

Is it? Cressida didn't sound impressed.

She headed back to the kitchen, crouched in front of Valentine's prone form and waved her bag of rich Goblin Blend coffee beans under the vampire's nose, a sure antidote to the sleeping draught her mother had slipped him.

Valentine blinked awake. "Why am I tied up?"

"How do you feel?"

"Awful…"

Same as he looks then.

"Maybe going to sleep broke the spell?" Fi said hopefully.

"Nobody can see my fantastic new clothes."

So much for that theory. "Valentine, you're not wearing any clothes. It's all an illusion."

The vampire frowned, his dark brows drawing together. Then he laughed. "You're hilarious. Of course I'm wearing clothes, you're just too stupid to see them. Only the cleverest people can see the fine threads."

Fi groaned. It was exactly like the children's storybook.

I said it wouldn't work.

"Not helpful, Cressida."

Valentine twisted, straining at his restraints and burst through the vines with a show of vampiric strength. Fi scrabbled backwards, shouting for her mum to help.

Valentine pushed himself to his feet, several leaves bunched around his waist, providing a much-appreciated service in the name of public decency. He raised one foot to start parading around the kitchen again, but his toe caught in a vine, and he toppled over, heading straight for Fi.

She closed her eyes as the leaves fell, raised her hands over her head and electricity crackled to cover her skin as the naked vampire collided with her in a tangle of limbs and leaves.

"Ouch! That's the second time you've used your magic on me. Why did you do that?"

"To stop you falling on me." Fi fought to push him off. Shocking him was instinct, her magic couldn't stop people colliding with her, but it could make them sorry that they had.

The vampire got to his feet and took in the kitchen. "Where am I? This isn't the café. And why am I naked?" He turned his back on Fi, facing the kitchen cupboard, the faintest smear of a blush tainting his pale skin.

"You picked up an enchanted jacket, young man. Stay there and I'll find you some clothes." Nell stalked off and returned a few long minutes later with some trousers and a shirt. It wasn't until much later that it occurred to Fi to wonder where her mum had got men's clothes from at such short notice.

Nell placed them on the side nearest the vampire and then stood with the table providing a barrier between them as Valentine tugged them on. Fi scooted backwards until her spine touched a wall and kept her hands over her eyes until he gave a polite cough.

"I'm decent. But I still don't understand."

Fi peeked through her fingers to make sure it was safe before she took her hands away from her face. "You were strutting around the café with nothing on. You really don't remember anything?"

He shook his head, his pale cheeks reddening further. "I didn't even know vampires could be enchanted."

"It takes a great deal of magic, but it can be done…" Nell said, tapping a long finger to her cheek.

"So, can I go?"

"I suppose… no, wait. What's the last thing you remember?" Fi recovered from the trauma of having a naked vampire in her kitchen enough to remember she was a Magical Liaison Office agent.

"I was in the café, helping tidy up. Someone had left a leather coat… I think I picked it up, I was going to put it on the coat rack…then I'm here. Where is here?"

"My house," Nell said, as if that explained anything.

Fi rolled her eyes at her mother's assumption that everyone knew who she was and where she lived. "And do you remember who left the jacket?"

The vampire shrugged. "No idea. I'd only just woken up. I wasn't exactly paying attention to the customers. I'll have to speak to the werewolf about extended opening hours if he wants me to be more help."

"And no one would want to cause you harm, or to look stupid?"

Valentine gave her a look, and his eyes flared red. "The people who wanted to cause me harm burned down my home. I don't think anyone other than you, the werewolf and the lady who owned the café even know I'm here."

Fi flinched. She hadn't made any progress finding out who had set the fire that destroyed the vampire's lair. "Yeah, sorry. I'll let you know when I find anything out." Fi knew it wasn't the right time, but she had to ask. "About the magic, did you…complain about me the first time I shocked you? Like an official complaint, I mean."

The vampire blinked at her. "Why would I complain? I don't want to get on the MLO's radar. It hurt like hell, but I heal fast. Besides, if you hadn't magicked me, I would have run, and we'd never have spoken, and I wouldn't have anywhere to live now my house has been destroyed." There was that hint of accusation.

"OK, sorry again. I'll be in touch about the fire."

Valentine nodded and swept out of the back door, clutching his new clothes to his body.

"At least we know how to break this enchantment," Nell said, her arms crossed.

Fi sighed and gathered the smallest prickle of electricity to her fingers; it was time to shock her supervisor.

Chapter 25

Ursula awoke with a cry as Fi touched her shoulder with a dusting of electricity. "What on earth was that for?"

"The coat enchanted you, and you started to strip, so we put you to sleep until we could break the spell."

"You drugged a superior officer?"

Cressida hissed at the accusation.

"Good thing we did, or you'd be waltzing around in the nuddy," Nell added.

"Yes, well." Ursula rebuttoned her cardigan. "Where is this coat?"

Fi retrieved it from the library, carefully picking it up with the tongs. As she lifted it, the book of fairy tales fell to the floor. Fi gathered it up and took it with her as she hurried back to the kitchen.

She dropped the coat on the large wooden table, wrinkling her nose at the stale charity shop smell. Ursula waved her hands over it, careful not to touch the worn leather, and wrinkled her brow.

"It's definitely enchanted, but I can't tell what it's supposed to do."

"It makes people think they're wearing clothes when they're naked."

"Why would anyone want to enchant something to do that?"

"Good question."

"Have you completed a report?"

Fi forced down her sigh. "I only just woke you up. I thought that was more important than paperwork."

Ursula thought for a moment, then nodded. "Righto, I'll come with you while you submit the report. Where's your office?"

Cressida snorted a laugh, and Fi glared at her.

"Er, I mostly work in my room, but I'll bring my laptop down here." She scurried off to retrieve the computer.

There was no way she wanted Ursula in her bedroom; there were still posters of videogames from her teenage years on the walls, when she'd thought that the cartoon women with large…assets, were cool instead of blatant objectification. Her fingers itched. She needed to do some stress baking tonight, or shoot something online.

When she returned to the kitchen, her mother had made a round of hot drinks and sat chatting to Ursula on the table. Fi plonked herself into a free chair on the other side of the agent and opened up the laptop to the MLO report page.

She filled out the sparse details that she had, grimacing as she referenced the fairy tale; it sounded stupid to her, and she was the one writing it. What she needed was to figure out why someone was causing chaos and what the shoe shop and the café had in common, because it seemed like the victims were picked at random.

She minimised the report and pulled up her virtual corkboard.

"What's that?" Ursula peered over her shoulder.

"Oh, it's just a programme I designed. It's like a detective's murder board. I find it useful for mapping out cases, it helps me find connections."

She tensed, expecting a tirade from the uptight agent, but Ursula said, "Interesting. How does it work?"

Fi began typing in virtual sticky notes and placing them on the board. She used the mouse to draw red lines between the shops and the victims, stopping to search online and on her phone for pictures to illustrate the notes. She paused and added the stories she thought were connected to the trouble, with more lines to the existing notes, and then added another sticky note full of questions: What did the victims have in common? Answer – nothing, apparently. What did the shops have in common? Who was powerful enough to perform the enchantments? And what was their motive? What did fairy tales have to do with anything?

Fi stopped and drummed her fingers on the table. She'd reached the extent of her knowledge.

"You should add on how to break the enchantments," Ursula encouraged.

Fi nodded and tapped out 'electricity' next to the jacket and 'take off shoes' next to the shoes.

"You should talk to the Office about this app. I think it could be useful for other agents too."

Fi nodded again; she'd had the same thought but had never got round to it. She scribbled a reminder on her phone.

"And you'll need to inform the police about the latest incident."

Fi pulled a face, but she dutifully emailed a copy of the report to Detective Ledd. At least he hadn't been involved first hand tonight. Fi couldn't imagine how things could get worse than a naked vampire in the kitchen, but she was sure they would have been if the detective had turned up.

Ursula stretched. "Lovely. I think that's all we can do tonight. Tomorrow, we'll have to interview the charity shop owner and that werewolf down at the café. Best get a good night's sleep. You did complete the report about the fire?"

Fi groaned and opened up another template. It was going to be a long night. The other witches left her to it and she filed the report for Valentine's house, requesting everything the police and the fire brigade had on the arson attack and attaching a photo of the hat.

She stretched. What a strange day it had been. She'd got more control of her magic than she'd had before, had dinner with her ex and managed to break the enchantments on the vampire and her supervisor. Fi reached for her phone, eager to share her day with Mort.

She paused, phone in hand. It was like a veil had lifted from her eyes as the realisation struck her; she wanted to share things with Mort.

Totally different to how it had been with Li. Fi felt free. She'd finally told Li that she didn't care and meant it. It was as if she had been upset he'd left her all this time because she felt she should have been upset, because her family had liked Li and settling down in a relationship was what you were supposed to do. It was totally different with Mort. She wanted to be with him. Her head jerked up as she processed that thought.

She wanted to spend time with Mort. She wanted to share things with him, but she had messed up when she'd ran away the other day. Hesitantly, she sent him a text asking if he had time to talk. He rang back moments later.

"Hi."

"Hi yourself. How's it going?"

"I just wanted to say sorry. I shouldn't have run out on you, but my ex called."

"Oh."

"Yeah, it's all over, but there's this case…"

"I understand. I'll give you some space to think things through. I'm on call tonight anyway…"

Fi winced. Even with her poor social skills, she knew she'd hurt him. "OK, I'll let you go then. Speak soon?"

"Whenever you're ready."

He hung up. Fi sighed. That had gone terribly. With a snort of frustration, she opened up her online gaming profile and logged in; she needed to shoot something.

Chapter 26

Fi stifled a yawn as she walked with Ursula to the local charity shop on the High Street. She hadn't heeded the older agent's advice to get an early night.

After filing the report for Valentine and talking to Mort, she had taken out some of her frustration with the case by blowing up aliens with her online friends. It was cathartic, but then she had read the book of fairy tales she'd taken from the library until she fell asleep, and she'd dreamed that she turned into a swan dancing in red shoes, trying to flee a beast chasing her through a castle until Cressida had woken her up and told her to keep it down.

She covered the next yawn with her hand. As she got older, staying up late had more serious consequences on her ability to focus the next day. Fortunately, there was always coffee. She nursed the travel mug of strong, black Goblin Blend coffee in her hand; the elixir of waking.

Ursula had no such problems and bounced along the pavement with a skip in her step. Fi wanted to believe that this meant things were going well and she wasn't in trouble, but she'd had enough performance assessments in her IT jobs to know that they rarely ended well for her. She sipped her coffee and stayed quiet, so she didn't interrupt her superior's good mood.

"Here we are." Ursula stopped outside the shop – *Goodwill Hunting* – and addressed Fi. "You take the lead in there. I'll look around and see if anything else is enchanted."

Fi nodded and stepped inside. The scent of pre-loved clothes washed over her, that strange, musty floral smell that reminded her of a granny's cupboard, even though she never remembered her own grandmother having anything that smelled like that. The array of clothes, jewellery and books overwhelmed her eyes, arranged by a mix of colour, length, and size. She could have sworn there was more stock in the small space than normal physics should allow.

A young man flapped a scarf and folded it before adding it to a shelf. He smiled at them and turned back to the box of clothes at his feet.

Fi stepped forward and coughed. "Will?" she asked, reading the name tag on his shirt.

He started and looked up, blinking as if he was unused to customers wanting to interact. "Can I help you with something?" His gaze flicked to Cressida. "Is that a dragon?"

Can no humans tell the difference between dragons and wyrms? Cressida's tail curved in annoyance.

"She's a wyrm and she's house trained."

Really!

Fi showed Will her Magical Liaison Office ID, placed the paper bag she carried on the counter, and shook out the leather jacket. "Someone bought this coat from your shop."

He reached out his hand.

"Don't touch it!"

"OK…" Will looked at Fi like she was insane. "But I need to check the label."

Fi withdrew the pastry tongs from the bag and opened the coat until the label was visible.

"Yes, that's from our shop. What's going on?"

"This jacket was used in a magical incident last night… where were you yesterday?"

He frowned, causing his piercings to jingle slightly. "I was here all day. A large donation came in just before four, so I stayed late to sort it, still going through it, as you can see." He gestured to the box by his feet. "And then I had a quick sandwich before heading to the magic club at the village hall."

Cressida sniffed the box and coughed. *It smells like something vomited in there.*

Fi ignored her familiar. "Aren't you a bit old to go to a kids' club?"

He guffawed, and his tongue piercing glinted. "I run it. After the previous leader was arrested, it seemed a shame to leave the kids with nothing to do. They all love the club."

Fi noted that down. She remembered the previous leader all too well. The woman had tried to channel a demon to protect the kids, and now that demon was trapped in a donkey grazing on her mother's lawn. "I'll check that out. Do you know who bought this coat?"

He shook his head. "We get a lot of people in here, but I might be able to tell you when it was bought, if I can scan the barcode?"

Fi nodded. That should be OK. "Just don't touch the coat."

The shop worker got up the details after a couple of beeps. "We sold this yesterday. That's all I can tell you."

"Do you have any CCTV?"

"Yes, I can dig out the footage."

"Great, I'll pick it up in an hour." Fi turned to Ursula, and the other agent nodded. "Did you find anything else?"

The weather witch shook her head. "Let's get to the café."

Chapter 27

After Fi had dropped her coat at the dry cleaners to get any naked vampire germs off it, they headed to the café. Fi asked for a refill of her coffee before she started interviewing Steve, while Ursula took a seat at an empty table with the coat back in its bag. Once she had her large americano in her hands and bacon cooking for her familiar, she asked Steve about the case.

"So, did you see who left the coat yesterday?"

The werewolf shook his head. "Sorry, there was a sudden rush at the end, a couple of late Halloween tourist groups turned up and the school kids were in here too. I was run off my feet, and the vampire didn't wake up in time to help, even though the sun was down." Steve raised his voice at the end as if Valentine could hear him grousing.

Fi groaned. She knew the shop didn't have any cameras. Effie relied on her magical barriers and wards to stop thieves, but if she was off travelling, they should really get some security. She doubted anyone would try to rob the shop. The muscular werewolf behind the counter was a decent deterrent for any would-be shoplifters, but it would be good to have footage of customers for occasions like this.

"And can you think of any reason someone might want to do this to you?"

"To me?" He frowned.

"Well, Valentine's only been here a couple of days and he sleeps all day so no one knows he's here. Maybe someone targeted you." It was a flimsy idea. After all, maybe whoever enchanted the jacket had meant to give it to someone else and had left it at the café by accident.

"Me? No. I get on with everyone, apart from the vampire, and only Glen is interested in seeing me naked."

Fi nodded, but from the way one of the mums sitting with their buggies at a nearby table eyed the werewolf, she wasn't sure that was true. Grabbing her drink and a cappuccino for Ursula, she retreated to their table.

"No leads here."

Ursula sighed and took a sip of her drink. "Well, we can hand the hat from the burned house to the police. Go on. Chop, chop."

Fi swallowed and made a call to Detective Ledd.

"Ledd here. What do you want?"

"I've got some evidence to hand in."

"Evidence? Have you got a lead on the shoes case?"

"Er, not exactly…did you get my report on the fire?"

"Yes, I saw that. And another enchantment in Omensford. Do you think they're connected?"

"Not sure, but I don't think so." Fi shook her head. She needed to get this exchange under control to impress Ursula. "But we checked out the house and found a hat. It might belong to whoever started the fire, so I need to hand it in." Great, she sounded like a schoolgirl handing in lost property.

"I've got someone in the area, I'll get them to pick it up. Call me when you have something concrete." He hung up.

"He sounded very efficient, and he listened to you. Must be useful working with a mundane who doesn't waste time."

Fi took a long sip of her coffee. Efficient was not one of the words she would choose to describe the stubborn detective.

Ursula checked her watch. "Let's get that video footage, hand over the hat, and get home."

Don't forget my bacon.

Chapter 28

In the back garden, Agatha stood barefoot next to Diane. A frown creased the young witch's face as she held her hands out towards the demon donkey. Fi's jaw dropped as Timaeus performed a dressage step.

"Wha–?"

"Hi Fi, how's it going? Diane's doing brilliantly, isn't she?" Agatha beamed at her protégé.

"Good, good. What is she doing?"

"Practicing her magic, of course."

"Is she *controlling* Timmy?"

"I'd say strongly suggesting…"

"Fascinating," Ursula said, pushing her glasses up her nose. "I thought you said that donkey was a demon."

"He is…was…is, sort of." Fi wasn't exactly sure what Timaeus was.

"Then that young witch is one to watch, there's not many magic users who can use suggestion over a demon."

Why don't you try to sense her magic? Cressida suggested, her tongue flicking out as if she was tasting the air.

Fi took a step closer and held out her hand, using the thin thread between her and Cressida to temper her own magic until she could feel the power emanating from Diane. It was a strange sensation, like hammers pounding nails into her palm. It was like the tiny flicker of enchantment she had sensed but magnified a hundred times and more painful than Ursula's weather magic. Fi drew her hand back with a yelp.

The noise broke Diane's concentration and Timaeus' eyes glowed. "What hath thee done, witchling?"

Diane burst into giggles and the others struggled to keep their faces straight.

The demon donkey's nostrils flared, and he charged towards them. The four witches and one wyrm fled inside the house, which slammed the door behind them.

"If I had my demon form, thee would be ashes and dust!" Timaeus brayed from the garden, the door thudding as he threw his donkey form against the house.

"You wound him up."

Diane shrugged, still grinning. "Yeah, but did you see?"

"Still," Agatha frowned, "maybe I let it go too far. You'd better avoid the garden for a while. We'll have to find somewhere else to practise your control."

"Maybe I could try on one of your coven..."

Agatha shook her head. "It's considered bad form to use mind powers on people without their consent. I'll talk to Liv and see what she did when she was learning to control her magic."

"But she's a dream witch," Fi interrupted.

"It's all mind related, just different branches, like how weather witches are a specialisation of nature witches with affinity for the weather."

"Cool." Fi hastily agreed, recognising that Agatha had slipped into teacher mode. She shook her hand, still stinging from Diane's mind magic, but she had to know. "Aggy, can you do some magic, so I can sense it?"

Agatha's lips moved into a small smile, unable to resist an opportunity to help someone learn. She walked over to the trailing pot plant in the kitchen and her fingers glowed green as she made the vines plait together neatly.

Fi moved closer and held out her other palm, focusing on keeping her magic contained by the familiar bond. Almost immediately, she sensed Agatha's power. It was like thorns pressing into her flesh.

"It might be easier to sense her magic because you're related."

Agatha agreed with Ursula. "And the more powerful the magic, the easier it is to sense, too."

"Still hurts though," Fi said, wiping her hand on her trousers, as if that would help stop the prickling sensation that ran up and down her palm, like she'd shoved her hand into a patch of stinging nettles.

"That's because my magic is different to yours. Magic of the same type is always a nicer sensation."

Great. Fi had never met another witch with electrical power, so it looked like any magic she sensed would always hurt.

"Don't be disheartened," Ursula said. "You two girls are different branches of the same family tree, that's all."

"Oh, leaf it out," Fi said with a smile, unable to resist a bad pun.

Her sister took the bait and replied with her own plant-based pun. "I can't be-leaf you would say that."

"Branch out with your jokes, would you?"

"Tree harder."

Both sisters dissolved into fits of giggles at the awful puns while the others stared at them as if they were mad. Maybe they were, but they always bonded over their shared love of simple wordplay.

Sometimes you behave like a child, do you know that?

Cressida didn't appreciate her sense of humour.

"Hey, I've got a copy of that book, found a first edition in a charity shop." Diane opened the book of fairy tales that Fi had left on the table, leafing through the pages. "It's so cool. I never knew all the stories were caused by magic users."

Fi mumbled something. 'Cool' was not how she'd describe the stories in that book; disturbing, maybe, but not 'cool'.

"What are you up to, anyway?" Agatha asked.

"Just solving cases, taking names."

"Is this about the naked man last night? That was totes hilarious." Diane snorted.

"How did you know about that?"

The young witch shifted her feet and looked down. "I was at the pub."

"OK, yes, it is about that, but I can't say any more. Private MLO business."

"So, you don't know who did it?" Agatha asked.

"We're getting close," Fi said.

"And you shouldn't be out drinking. What would your mother say?" Agatha said to Diane.

"Sorry, Mrs Blair. Please don't tell Mum."

Agatha sighed. "I won't, this time. If you promise not to practise on people."

"Cross my heart."

"OK then. I heard it didn't go so well with Fi-Li…" Agatha changed topic so suddenly that Fi blinked as she caught up.

Cressida hissed her disapproval at the mention of Fi's ex.

"How did you know about that?"

"Mum."

Typical. Fi sighed. "I walked out on him."

"Who's Li?" Diane asked, her head cocked to one side.

"Her ex. And good for you."

"He wants to move to Omensford."

Agatha pulled a face.

As if they'd summoned him, Li walked into the kitchen. Ursula took a sip of tea, like this was her own private soap opera.

"What are you doing here?" Fi folded her arms and glared as Li invaded their private space.

Cressida growled and bared her teeth.

"Well, if you hadn't stormed out at dinner, I'd have had a chance to tell you I'm staying here while I look for places in the town."

Fi forced herself to breathe. It was a free country. He could stay in her mother's B&B. But this bit of the house was out of bounds for guests.

"What are you doing in the kitchen?"

"I wanted a spare pillow."

"I'll get you one." Fi led the way to the linen cupboard and selected the lumpiest pillow she could find.

"Have you thought about what I said?" he asked.

"No, Li. I have a job with responsibilities and, as I said, I don't care what you do or where you live. But you're not having my house. Now leave me alone." Fi slammed the door shut and shoved the pillow into Li's arms.

She whirled and almost ran into Diane.

"Sorry, just needed the bathroom," Diane said, hiding a smirk. Great. She had heard everything.

"Come on, Li was just going to bed."

Something tugged at Fi's unconscious, but she was so keen to get away from her ex that she dragged Diane back to the kitchen.

Diane shuffled on her feet. "Have we got much more training today? The school dance is this evening, and I promised my friends I'd help them get ready. Gill's really worried about her spots."

"Come on, I'll walk you out. I know how important these dances are." Agatha's eyes turned misty with fond memories of her youth.

Fi made a face, she never enjoyed those forced social situations where she ended up stuck in the corner. The best dance she'd been to as a teenager was the one where she'd persuaded the teachers to let her be the light technician.

It had gone great, and she'd used her magic to coax the machine into performing amazing feats of lighting that matched the mood of the music…until she'd shorted out the machine and blown a fuse, so everyone had to go home early. Still, she had spent the rest of her evening stripping down an old computer and rebuilding it, so she'd had a great time.

Fi retrieved the book from the table, left her sister to it and headed upstairs with Cressida to watch the footage, so caught up in her twisting thoughts about how the enchantments connected that she didn't notice Ursula following behind. The senior agent let out a gasp as Fi pushed her door open.

<h1 align="center">Chapter 29</h1>

"What is this?"

"Er, my room. Sorry, it's a bit messy."

A bit messy? Cressida snorted. *A family of trolls could be living here, and you'd never know.*

"It's not that bad…" Fi dumped the book on the bed and scrabbled around, picking clothing and tissues off the floor. It wasn't that bad really. The house would let her know when it got truly awful, usually by shaking the room until she cleaned it.

Fi finished by clearing a space on the bed and gestured that Ursula should sit. The agent looked dubious, but she perched on the edge of the bed, clutching her bag tightly on her lap. Cressida curled up in her usual spot and closed her eyes.

Fi searched in her pocket for the USB drive that the shop worker had given them and plugged it into her laptop. She opened up the file, and both witches watched as the screen filled with grainy black and white footage. A single customer entered the shop, browsed, then left again. Fi groaned. This would take forever. She fast forwarded the video, and the figures darted across the screen in comedic jerky motions at double speed.

The feed jumped between two cameras; one angled at the till and the other taking a wide view of the shop, but it wasn't high quality. Customers were practically indistinguishable from each other, and it was anyone's guess what they were buying.

"There, go back."

Fi squinted at the screen and rewound the footage before playing it at normal speed. A group of youths swarmed into the shop. Nothing unusual there, but, Ursula was right, they were spending a lot of time next to the coat section. One of them selected a jacket while others picked through the racks of clothes.

"Maybe one of them bought it, but this isn't exactly hard evidence."

"True, but maybe we can ask that young lady your sister is training if she recognises any of them. There's only one secondary school in the town, so she might know someone."

"Maybe…" It sounded tenuous to Fi, but she didn't have any other ideas. She attached the footage to the report and sent another copy to Detective Ledd, playing by the rules of prompt paperwork while the other agent supervised.

She drummed her fingers on the desk. "What do we do now?"

"I don't know about you, but I need a cup of tea. I'll see you downstairs for dinner, your mother mentioned a stew…"

Fi nodded. "I'll be down later, I think I'll catch up on some reading." She waited for Ursula to leave before opening a new window on her browser.

The complaint still bothered her and she could only think of one person who would have complained.

She typed the name into the search engine and was rewarded with the ugly face of Finn O'Riley at anti-magic protests, anti-magic rallies, anything against magic users.

Fi drummed her fingers against the desk. It would be oh so easy to make his life hard online, a quick hack here, a click there and he would be on several government lists.

Her fingers itched, and she forced her hands into balls to stop herself. She couldn't cross that line. She worked for a government department. Even if he was an arse. And Ursula wasn't that bad, a bit annoying to have someone breathing down her neck and insisting on reports being filled out, but it wasn't like she was fired. Not yet, anyway. And she'd learned loads about her magic, so it hadn't all been bad.

She clutched her mouse to close the window when she saw a splash of red. Frowning, she enlarged the picture of O'Riley at a recent protest in London. He sported a red hat…was that a coincidence?

Fi copied the picture and the link to the site into the report on the arson attack, maybe the police would find some DNA and O'Riley would get some karma.

Before she was tempted to do more, she pushed away from the desk and slumped onto the bed, picking up the book of fairy tales that lay discarded on her covers. "These ought to be called witch tales. They're all about magic users misusing their power, not the fae folk."

Some magic users think they are above mundane humans.

Something in Cressida's tone made Fi pause. She looked over the top of the red backed book. "And you?"

I...used to think that magic users were better than others, special somehow, but now...working with you...I've seen some of the things magic users do, and they're not all benevolent, like Goody.

Fi ignored the comment about Cressida's former owner. Not everyone had considered Goody to be a good witch; her mother for example. "Magic users are still people."

Exactly. People with the potential for great good or great evil.

"The ones in these stories are definitely evil, it seems like all they did was go around abusing people."

The wyrm shifted on the bed. *The tales are lessons to stop magical beings misusing their powers. Some of those stories are exaggerated.*

Fi wasn't sure about that, but she shut up and went back to reading, an uneasy feeling settling in her stomach. She was unsure how she felt about being linked to a familiar who believed in magical supremacy, even if the wyrm had changed her mind. But then, it wasn't like Fi was perfect. She turned the page and began reading about a warlock who enchanted a flower to put people to sleep, when her phone rang.

"Aggy?"

"Come quick! Emergency!"

Chapter 30

Fi ran down the stairs, clutching Cressida under one arm and juggling her phone in the other hand. Her sister was terrified, and that was all she needed to know, but she caught garbled words about enchantments and necklaces. She stuffed her feet into her faded converse trainers and grabbed her vacuum cleaner from the cupboard under the stairs.

"What's going on?" Ursula asked, midway through pouring tea from a teapot into a delicate cup painted with dancing cats. It looked like her mother trusted her enough to make a proper cup of tea.

"Diane and her friends are in trouble – enchanted necklace – I'm heading there now – no time."

"I'm coming with you."

Fi frowned, unsure if her X-5000 could hold two people and a wyrm, but there wasn't time to dawdle. She grabbed the vacuum, raced outside and told the older witch to grab on as she trickled some of her power into the machine and angled it up towards the sky. She kicked off and, with a protesting whine from the X-5000, they were airborne.

"You know, you really should learn to drive…" That was the last Fi heard as they zoomed into the air with the full power of cyclone technology propelling them onwards.

The wind whipped around them, forcing them forwards, and Fi wondered if Ursula was using her power as they flew. She opened her mouth to ask, but the air choked her and she closed it again, gripping the handle and leaning over to protect Cressida from the gale.

Fi poured as much magic as she dared into the vacuum, willing it to go faster while knowing that if she blew the fuse, they would all plummet to the ground and never make it to the teenagers. They crossed Omensford in record time and Fi angled the X-5000 into a nosedive, pulling up at the last second for a bumpy landing in someone's front garden.

I hate flying. Cressida shook out her small wings.

Fi ignored the irony of a creature with wings hating to fly and scanned the street, searching for house numbers on the carbon copy Cotswold stone clad houses on the estate.

"What are we looking for?"

"Number twelve."

"There." Ursula pointed, and they sprinted to a house with an open door, spilling light out onto the paved pathway.

"Aggy?"

"Is that you? Up here." The edge of panic in her sister's voice had Fi racing up the carpeted stairs two at a time.

"Thank goddess you're here. Quick." Agatha bent over a prone teenage girl, clawing at her neck. A large emerald pendant hung from a gold chain looped around her throat. As they watched, the chain twisted back on itself, cutting into her delicate skin.

"What happened?" Fi asked as Ursula bent over the girl.

"Diane called me. Her friend put on this necklace, and it started choking her. They couldn't get it off. But this is beyond me. I called you as soon as I got here."

The girl on the floor gasped out a rattling breath as her fingernails dug into her skin. Fi joined Ursula on the floor and looped her fingers around the metal chain, tugging at the necklace.

"It's no good. I can't break it. Whatever curse is on this necklace must prevent it from breaking."

Fi's mind raced. "Maybe we can just take it off. Like the shoes." She fed the chain through her hand, searching for a clasp and swore. It was just a loop of chain, one that had wound itself too tight to slip back over the girl's head.

"It's OK, sweety." Agatha took hold of the teenager's hand and soothed her.

Fi concentrated on the necklace. All the comforting words in the world wouldn't save the kid if they couldn't get the necklace off or break the enchantment. "I'm going to try something. Cressida, I need your help."

The wyrm was at her side in an instant. Fi placed one palm on the small creature's warm scales and the other on the large star-shaped pendant hanging from the necklace. She closed her eyes and pushed on the thread of the familiar bond, letting Cressida take some of the strain of her magic so she could let the tiniest dribble out onto the necklace.

The teenager screamed; it came out as a rasping noise that sounded like a hedgehog in distress. Fi swore again as the chain tried to twist tighter. The tech witch shoved her fingers under the necklace, prising the chain away from the girl's reddened skin and forcing the twisting golden chain apart. Her skin turned white as the chain bit into her fingers.

She winced at the pain and tried to think. Shocking the necklace hadn't broken the enchantment like it had with Valentine, and they couldn't remove it like they had with the shoes… "We need to cut the chain. Ursula, see if they have any tools here. Agatha and I will try to stop the necklace from tightening."

Her supervisor nodded and raced off, while the other two witches strained against the twisting chain. Ursula burst back into the room with a kitchen knife.

"That's not going to work! Get a hand here while I make a call." Fi waited until Ursula's fingers slipped under the chain, before pulling out her phone.

"Mort!"

"Great to hear from—"

"Sorry, but there's no time. I need you to bring your sword and get here now."

"I can help," Ursula said from her spot by the girl.

"Ursula will pick you up. Be ready." She hung up and turned to the older witch. "Do you need my vacuum?"

The agent shook her head. "I'm a weather witch. I can get there quicker riding the wind. It's not comfortable or convenient like a broomstick, but it's fast. Now take my place and give me the address."

Fi leaned back as she gave the address and garbled directions before grimacing as the chain wound more tightly around the girl's neck and her fingers. Ursula dashed downstairs.

"Tell mum and dad I love them," the girl croaked between shaky breaths.

"Hush now, save your strength for when we get you out of this," Agatha said.

Fi tried to smile.

Stop grimacing, you'll scare the girl.

The tech witch grabbed the knife. She had to feel like she was doing something active. Futilely, she sawed at the links, not even denting the enchanted metal as she strained with her other hand, leaning her entire body into stopping it from twisting further.

Chapter 31

Mort entered the room with the presence of a minor god, his face darkened with strange shadows and more angular than Fi remembered.

"Oh no, you are not taking her life," Agatha shouted at him from her spot on the floor.

He knelt next to her. "I'm not here for that. What do you need?"

"The sword. You have to cut the necklace."

He nodded and drew the blade. The girl's eyes widened, and she struggled to get away from the tall man with the sword. Agatha and Fi leaned back as the necklace took advantage of the struggle to twist itself into another knot.

"It's OK, he's here to help. Quickly!"

Taking the sword in his hands, he used the very tip to nick through the chain as if it were a delicate thread. The necklace fell to the floor and Agatha and Fi tumbled backwards from the sudden release of pressure on their hands.

Fi prodded the necklace cautiously with the knife, but it lay flat on the floor, the enchantment broken. She picked up the pieces as Agatha comforted the girl and helped her up to the bed.

Fi left them and headed down the stairs, making it to the bottom just as a dishevelled woman entered through the front door and stared around the house.

"What's happening? I got a call about Gill. Who are you?"

"Er, I'm Fiona, a Magical Liaison Office agent. A necklace tried to choke your daughter, but she's OK now."

"What?!"

Ursula appeared at the bedroom doorway and shot Fi a look before she called the woman upstairs, explaining the situation.

Mort and Fi stood in the hall. She fingered the pieces of the necklace in her pocket and reached out with her new ability to sense magic. Her heart sank as she found a familiar trace of magic that pressed like a tapping hammer against her palm, pricking her skin.

Oh no…

"What's wrong?" Agatha asked as she descended the stairs.

"You might want to come with me for this, Aggy. Sorry Mort, I'll talk to you later."

"I'll be here for you," he said.

Fi squeezed his hand then turned to her familiar. "Cressida, lead the way."

Chapter 32

The two sisters followed the golden wyrm out into the back garden. They headed towards the sound of sobbing to a wooden arbour where the girl sat.

"Diane…" Fi started.

"I didn't mean to!" she sobbed.

"What?" Agatha looked between the two. "Oh no, you didn't…"

"I wanted to help."

Fi took a spot next to the distraught teenager while Agatha sat on her other side, hesitating between offering comfort and scolding the child.

"What did you do?"

"Gill said she wanted to look good for the dance. She's been trying to impress Roman since forever, and so I said that I'd help. I've been practising my enchantments, and I'm good…"

Both sisters pursed their lips in twin expressions of distaste, but it was Fi who spoke. "How did you end up strangling her?"

"Is she…did I kill her?"

A fresh wave of tears washed over the girl, and Agatha pulled her close. "No, she's alive and she'll be fine, but you need to be honest with us. What did you do?"

"I put an enchantment on the necklace to make her this beautiful forever – it should have been fine. I don't understand why it went wrong – but the chain started twisting and choking her and I panicked and I couldn't get the spell off – everything I tried made it worse and the others were screaming and that's when I called you…"

Agatha patted her back and exchanged a look with her sister.

"Did you get the idea from the book of fairy tales?" Fi asked.

Diane sniffed and nodded. "It was a bit of fun, that's all. The copy I got in the charity shop had a load of notes in it and I tried some small things and they worked, then that snooty lady in the shoe shop kicked us out, so I enchanted the shoes before we left. I didn't mean for anyone to get hurt, I had it under control."

"The woman who tried on the shoes is still in hospital," Fi said.

Diane buried her face against Agatha's plump shoulder.

"And the jacket?" Fi asked.

"Gill dared me to; she thought it would be funny to get Steve to streak through the town…"

"So, you wanted to humiliate him?"

"No! It was just a bit of fun."

"This is serious Diane; I've got to take you into custody. There's a reason those fairy tales are in the past. Attacking mundanes like that is against the law."

"Fi... she's a minor..."

"She almost killed someone. This is out of my hands." Seeing the distress on her sister's face and Diane's guilt-wracked expression, Fi sighed and rubbed her forehead. "But I'll see what I can do."

Ursula strode across the neatly mowed lawn. "The doctor said you'd be out here. What's going on?"

Fi took a deep breath and stood while Diane sobbed behind her, and Agatha made gentle shushing noises. Sometimes she thought her sister could sympathise with an axe murderer.

"We found the culprit behind the enchantments." Fi jerked a thumb over her shoulder at the teenager and Ursula blinked owl-like behind her large glasses.

"It wasn't ill intentioned for the most part, more stupidity than anything else and she's a minor...is there anything we can do?" Fi asked.

Ursula pursed her lips so tightly that they turned white. "That sort of power without proper restraint can be deadly to our society. She could have damaged the fragile relationship between magical beings and mundane humans if this had gone any further..."

Fi led her to one side and lowered her voice. "Come on, didn't you do anything stupid when you were a teenager?"

The older agent's lips twitched, and her eyes softened as if at a fond memory. She nodded and turned back to the distraught girl. "But, at the Magical Liaison Office, we don't like to punish children…I could recommend an apprenticeship with another witch with similar powers."

Diane perked up and stared up at the two agents with large, tear-filled eyes.

"With regular check ins, of course, and your power will be bound until we can trust you, we can't risk anything like this happening again."

Fi shuddered at the mention of binding magic. Separating a magic user from their powers was almost the worst thing that could happen to a magical being. Even though she hated her electrical magic at times, and it caused her more problems than she could count, it was part of her, as integral to her as a motherboard was to a computer, and she couldn't imagine life without it.

But the teenager nodded. "Anything, I'll do anything, just please, don't send me to prison."

Ursula gave a curt nod. "Lovely. Well then, we'd better go and tell your parents."

Diane stood, wiping her face and streaking thick globs of mascara over her cheeks. "Mrs Blair, please, will you come with me?"

"Of course, little one."

"No time like the present." Ursula led the way across the garden.

Diane turned. "I really am sorry," she said. "Your ex…"

Fi frowned. What about Li? She rang the house and her mum picked up.

"Is Li alright?"

"Of course he is."

"Not cursed, or dead?"

"Of course not. The house would let me know. The last time someone died here, it was so embarrassed it made the room off limits. It won't happen again."

"OK, be back soon. Wait, is that why that door in the hall won't open?"

But her mother had hung up.

Fi shivered and watched Diane go, crossing her arms around her body. That had been too close, a girl had almost been killed and she had been powerless to stop it. She'd had to rely on someone else…and it had turned out alright. She smiled and headed to the front of the house.

"Mort?"

He stepped out from the shadows.

"Thank you for coming."

"Of course, I'll always be here for you." He tucked a strand of hair behind her ear and Fi leaned her face against his palm.

"Sorry."

"For what?"

"For being flaky, for running out the other day. I just…needed time."

"I will always give you space. I don't want you to feel trapped."

Fi looked up into his chocolate brown eyes then to his lips. "I know what I want now," she whispered.

Mort stilled, and his gaze darted to her eyes as he waited.

"I want us. If you still want me, that is." Fi gave him an out, not sure if she had pushed him away too much, like she had with Li. She didn't care about her ex anymore, but she didn't want to repeat her mistakes, not with Mort, not when she had found someone who respected her space and didn't resent her for it, someone she could rely on completely.

After a long beat, he smiled and pulled her into a kiss. "I want you."

She should have left it there, but she had to know. Fi felt Cressida press against her calf, and she reached out with her magic to sense Mort's power. It was a heady rush of ecstasy, of something glorious and out of this world, before intense pain stabbed through her hand and she pulled away, clutching her palm.

"Fi? What happened?"

"I tried to sense your magic."

"And?" He was curious.

"I think we should stick to kissing."

Chapter 33

Fi yawned in perfect unison with her familiar, then smiled. "Maybe we are more in sync."

Maybe we're both tired after last night's exploits.

The tech witch agreed and took a large swig of her sweetened black coffee and a large bite of her hot buttered toast. The doorbell rang with the tune of Please Mr Postman and Fi went to answer the door with a roll of her eyes. Sometimes the house had a strange sense of humour.

She didn't recognise the delivery man, but she signed for the long package and brought it through into the kitchen where Ursula and her mother stood chatting.

"Er, this came for you, Mum."

Nell took the brown paper package with a frown. "I didn't order anything."

"No, I did. Go on, open it." A hesitant smile played on Ursula's lips as Nell carefully untied the string and unwrapped the brown paper to reveal a brand-new broomstick.

"Ursula, I don't know what to say…"

Fi's mouth dropped. Her mother was speechless.

"I'm so sorry I broke your broom. Again."

"It's forgotten."

They hugged and Fi grabbed a piece of toast from the table before she noticed the suitcase floating on a small cloud near the back door.

"You're leaving?" Fi asked through a mouthful of toast.

Ursula nodded. "I've seen enough. I'll write up my report and submit it to Agent Jones tomorrow."

Fi swallowed. "And?"

"I'll put it all in the report, but from what I've seen, you're a competent agent with growing control over her power. I'm recommending daily practice and regular training sessions, and you need to keep on top of your paperwork, but I'm confident you'll do well at the MLO. Just make sure you sort out the work situation at the café – you need permission if you get paid for your work."

Fi's shoulder's relaxed. "Thank you, thank you so much. Yes, I will. Thank you."

"Just doing my job, and it was nice to come back home and see friends." She smiled at Nell and embraced the other witch again. Her mother returned her hug stiffly, but there was a curve to her lips as she pulled away.

"Are you sure I can't tempt you with breakfast before you go?" Nell asked.

"No, thank you, I've got to pick up Diane and get to the head office as soon as possible. The powers that be don't like powerful witches roaming around rogue, especially ones who have caused as much trouble as that young witch."

"At least let me make you a hot drink."

The agent smiled. "A tea, please. Hardly anyone brews the leaves anymore."

Fi rolled her eyes; soaking a tea bag was so much quicker and she couldn't taste the difference, but her mum went to work with the teapot and loose leaves. Fi pushed the toast rack towards Ursula. Her mum couldn't make a cup of tea in less than five minutes, so the agent definitely had time for something to eat.

Ursula selected a slice and ate standing up, catching every single crumb on the white plate. Fi was impressed.

All too soon, she had a travel mug of tea in her hand and was ready to go.

"Thank you so much for having me. It's been lovely. Nell, we'll have to catch up sooner next time."

"It was far too long," her mother replied, embracing the stocky agent.

Ursula walked out of the door. Fi swallowed her toast and ran after her.

"Wait!"

"Yes?"

"Tell me something about mum before you go."

Ursula stared at her.

"Please, something that she wouldn't have told me."

The corners of the older witch's lips turned upwards, and she exchanged a look with Nell over Fi's shoulder. "Well…you didn't hear it from me, but there was this time when we dared her to ride her broomstick through the town naked during a full moon…"

Fi ignored the tsking noise her mother made behind her back. "And?"

"She did it! But she didn't want anyone to see her, so she spelled the whole town, apart from her coven, to make sure they were asleep!"

"What?!"

"Of course, we hounded her for months to find out how she did it, but she never revealed her secret. We suspect she slipped something into the water, but," she raised a shoulder, "we'll never know."

Fi gaped after the agent as she walked down the path. Well, she had some gossip for Agatha.

"Don't believe everything you hear."

"So, it isn't true?"

"I didn't say that…" her mother sashayed back into the house, a small smile curving her pink lips.

Back inside, Fi almost bumped into Li who yawned.

"Bad night?"

"The bed was so uncomfortable, it was like there was a lump in it everywhere I moved."

Fi frowned. The beds in the B&B were always comfy. A suspicion formed in her mind.

"Anyway, I spoke to Rhia and we think we might get a place in Spain instead. There was some weird weather last night – like a gale force wind. That's the problem with England. You can't guarantee the sun even in the summer."

"Good, that's good. You go have breakfast; I've just got to…"

Fi raced upstairs and, once she heard the click of the guest dining room door, went to Li's room.

The house let her in and she shuddered at the cold, starkness of the room with a huge ugly painting dominating one wall. The house changed its décor to suit the occupant, and this fit Li's overbearing personality to a tee.

With another glance at the door, she hurried over to the bed and rifled under the mattress until she found it. A pea. Enchanted. She shook her head. Another of Diane's pranks. That was what felt off when she handed Li the pillow. Diane hadn't come from the bathroom, but from Li's room. But Fi wasn't sorry her ex had had a dreadful night's sleep. Goodness knows she'd lost enough sleep worrying about him and how he'd react to some imagined slight.

And now he was getting a place in Spain, so she didn't have to worry about bumping into him in Omensford.

Her phone chirped and she read the text from Detective Ledd that they'd found a DNA match for the red hat and were making an arrest today. Whistling, she went downstairs to find Cressida and continue their practice through the familiar bond.

Epilogue

"Alright, based on Agent Fortescue's assessment and your commitment to continue with training sessions and attend a sensitivity seminar for interactions with the general public, I think we can close this complaint down."

Fi released the breath she had been holding. "Thank you, thank you so much."

Agent Jones held up her hand to stop Fi's babbling. She turned to the HR representative sitting in on the session. "Have you got all that?"

"Yes'm."

"And I'd also like it stated for the record that the complainant is under arrest for arson at this time."

"Yes'm. We've taken that into consideration and agree with your assessment. We're closing the complaint and removing it from Ms Blair's record."

"Good. You can go." Agent Jones leaned back in her chair and waited until the door clicked shut behind the hapless HR representative, then she speared Fi with her amber eyes. "And on a personal note, having investigated the complainant, I'd like to say that O'Riley sounds like a total dzraker, and I'm surprised we haven't been asked to investigate him before. He's on my watch list now, though. And he's got a court date for setting the fire at the vampire's place."

Fi's mouth dropped open at the Dwarfish swearword. "So, I'm not in trouble?"

The shifter shook her head. "From everything I've seen, you're doing a good job, and Agent Fortescue confirmed it. But you have to keep up with that dzraking paperwork."

"Yes, boss."

"Trust me, if you don't, it'll come back to bite you on the arse."

"Yes, boss."

"Stop 'yes, bossing' me. And take a holiday every once in a while."

"Er, yes boss."

"Alright, you can go. I've got to see a wizard about an invisibility cape. Some women have complained he hid in their changing room at the gym." She looked down at another file on the leather-topped desk and Fi stood, unable to stop a grin spreading across her face. She was doing a good job.

She strode out of Agent Jones' office with her head held high and beamed at the other agents in the main oddly angled room. It was a pentagon shape, but the angles were wrong, and it was bigger than it should have been. Two of the walls were lined with floor to ceiling bookcases that held concealed doors, crafted to blend in with the leatherbound books, it reminded her of the library back home, except these didn't drift away from their shelves and rearrange themselves.

Another wall held a massive flatscreen tv, a stark contrast to the mounted weapons on the adjoining wall. She ignored it all, a new confidence straightening her spine. The agents gave her some strange looks, but she didn't care. Maxi stopped her as she passed his messy desk, piles of paperwork and odd parts of machines covering the entire surface.

"How did it go?"

"Good. She said I was doing a good job." The words sounded strange in her mouth. No boss had ever told her that in her tech roles, unless it was to add a 'but' to the end of the sentence.

His eyebrows threatened to disappear beneath his floppy hair. "High praise indeed. She must really like you, Fifi."

"And she told me I need to take a holiday."

Maxi's blue eyes widened into saucers. "She's a fine one to talk. She barely takes any time off, unless it's to head to her family farm."

Fi shrugged.

"Fancy a coffee before you head back to the old village? I know a great little place in one of the arcades, and I've been working on a battery that can store magic, I thought you might want to experiment, yah?"

She shook her head. "Not right now, I've got a long journey back and I've got a hot date tonight."

He pulled her into an awkward hug and let her go. "See you around, Fifi."

***

An hour's train journey and another hour on a bus later, and Fi was back home. She couldn't keep the grin off her face. Mort was going to be so surprised. She packed the console and two controllers into a rucksack covered with pin badges and headed for the back door.

Glad you're finally seeing sense.

Fi shrugged her shoulders, then readjusted the bag on her back. "It took me long enough, but I'm taking a chance with Mort. Do you want to come along?"

The wyrm shook her head and snuggled back down in her cushion by the oven.

No thanks, I don't want to be a third wheel to you two snuggling all night.

Fi bit her lip. Maybe she should bake something to take with her.

Just go.

Cressida was right, she needed to stop thinking and trust her heart for once. "Thanks. You're pretty wise, you know that?"

I know.

Fi grinned and headed for the door. She paused at the threshold. The backpack was heavy and Mort lived on the other side of town…With a sigh, she retrieved her X-5000 vacuum cleaner from the cupboard. She mounted the cleaning machine, allowed a small amount of her magic to trickle into the vacuum and kicked off, hearing the heavy door creak shut behind her. The wind whistled around the witch as she flew over Omensford.

The town looked cosy with its twinkling lights in the dark evening, and then she was flying over the darker outskirts with fewer streetlamps. She found Mort's bungalow and touched down on the lawn, her shoes scudding on the dewy grass.

She paused outside the door, one hand hovering over the doorbell. Was this the right thing? What if Mort rejected her? Maybe it was better to live without trying to form a connection with someone else; she'd always done well on her own. Well, she'd done OK on her own.

But then, she hadn't been truly alone; her family had always been there for her, in their own way, and her online friends.

As if she could hear Cressida's voice sounding in her head, she pressed the bell and waited.

No turning back now.

Besides, she'd promised she was in this relationship, and she didn't go back on her word. She wasn't running away from this.

Mort appeared moments later, clad in a black turtleneck sweater that hugged his body.

"Hi."

He grinned. "Hi yourself."

"You owe me a date." Not the best declaration of affection, but her mouth was dry, and she had lost all her words.

"True. Did you have anything in mind?" He still had a smile on his face. That was a good sign.

She shrugged off the backpack and pulled out a controller. "I thought we could have a quiet evening in."

"Sounds perfect. Come on in."

He reached for the backpack like a gentleman, and her fingers tingled where his hand touched hers. Yes, she had made the right decision. She was going to enjoy this relationship, wherever it went. It was worth taking the risk.

Thank you

A special thank you to my amazing patrons: Emma Ward and Mark Canty who always supports me.

If you want to support Gemma, you can find her on www.patreon.com/G_Clatworthy for exclusive first reads of new stories.

You can also join her newsletter at www.gemmaclatworthy.com for a free prequel to her Rise of Dragons series and follow Gemma on www.instagram.com/gemmaclatworthy, www.facebook.com/gemmaclatworthy or join the Facebook reader's group Gemma's book wyrms.

Other Books by G Clatworthy

Books in the Rise of the Dragons series:

Awakening

Solstice of Dragons

Equinox Betrayal

Darkest Deception

Attack on Avalon

Fated Bloodlines

Books in the Omensford series (set in the Rise of the Dragons universe):

Bedsocks and Broomsticks

Cream Teas and Crystal Balls

Donkeys and Demons

Pumpkins and Popstars

Exes and Enchantments

Fae and Familiars

Children's Books

The Child Who series:

The Girl Who Lost Her Listening Ears

The Boy Who Lost His Listening Ears

The Girl Who Dreamed of Sleep

The Boy Who Dreamed of Sleep

Nanny Pastry series:

Nanny Pastry and the Nimble Ninjabread Man

Other books:

Coronavirus in the words of children

About the Author

Gemma started writing during the 2020 lockdown and loves fantasy fiction and dragons in particular. She lives in Wiltshire with her family and two cats and also enjoys crafts of all kinds. You can see all her writing on www.patreon.com/G_Clatworthy. Join the conversation at Gemma's book wyrms readers' group on Facebook.

She also writes children's books. You can find out more on her website www.gemmaclatworthy.com or follow her on Instagram (www.instagram.com/gemmaclatworthy) or Facebook (www.facebook.com/gemmaclatworthy).